瞬間理解英文閱讀

★陳 頎 著

書泉出版社 印行

自序 PREFACE

筆者從事多年的英文教育，深覺國人的英文能力不但沒有明顯的成長，反而往往有每況愈下的感覺。臺灣在國際化的驅使下，學習者應該有更多的英語學習動力。因此，英文有時學不好，也許是方法不對或是沒有使用到正確且實用的教材。

有同學常問我：「為什麼學了好多年的英語，英文單字一背就忘，英文閱讀的速度無法提升，甚或是一碰到外國朋友必須開口說英語的時候，卻又啞口無言？」其實，英語聽說讀寫四種能力的提升是有待平時的練習，而這類的練習應是反覆的、持續的與不間斷的。

筆者以過去的教學經驗，結合各項英文檢定考試（托福、雅思、多益、全民英檢和基測學測等）的發展趨勢， 撰寫本書。殷切期盼能以本書來強化學習者的閱讀能力與英文字彙的增進，並幫助廣大學子與考生，順利通過各種英文檢定考試。在此感謝書泉出版社所給予的協助。本書雖精心編校，但疏漏難免，尚請讀者們不吝賜教。

目錄 CONTENTS

PART 1 〉閱讀技巧實力提升

PART 2 〉閱讀測驗實戰練習

ONE

PART 1

閱讀技巧實力提升

Chapter 1

閱讀的字彙力

英文的學習者常常會問：「為何我的閱讀速度不夠快，導致很多的閱讀考試都來不及寫完，導致考試的分數過低，亦或是就算是一整句的英文單字我都懂，但是加起來成為一句時，我又都看不懂，或是不了解作者的意思。」這是一般英文閱讀者的疑惑與通病。其實閱讀的速度不夠快，百分之七十是因為讀者本身單字量的問題，一句話裡頭若出現五個以上或是多個我們所謂的「生字」時，就容易導致閱讀的中斷。但是單字這麼多，我們應該如何著手，以最短的時間獲得最快以及最大的效果呢？本章我們先要了解一些單字的理解方式，由「字」而「句」，再由「句」而「文」，讓你迅速累積大量的單字，並快速破解所有文章裡頭的字彙與文句。

1.1 字首、字根與字尾的概念

字首、字根與字尾是學習單字的必要方式，了解其中的概念對於單字的理解或是對於一個新的「生字」的「猜測」有絕對的幫助，這也就是為何一般留學補習班在教導字彙學習時都會特別指導。在學過這方面的概念後，對於一些留學考試如托福(TOFEL)、雅思(IELS)，或是證照考試如新多益(TOEIC)或是全民英檢(GEPT)，有分數大幅提升的幫助。以下精選實用的重點式的字、字根、字尾。我們先來看看以下的這個單字：

autobiography

auto_bio_graphy

auto是「自己」或是「自動」的意思，例如：automatic自動的 / autonomy自治權；bio是「生命」的意思，例如：biology生物學 / bioengineering生物工程學；graphy是「寫字」或「紀錄」意思，例如：photography攝影 / geography地理學。

所以，autobiography是「寫自己的生命」，也就是「自傳」的意思！

高頻率常用的字首

Prefixes	Meaning	Examples
After-	**After**	**Aftermath** **Afterward**
Ante-	**Before or in front of**	**Antecessor** **Antenatal**
Anti-	**Against**	**Antibody** **Antibiotic**
Auto-	**Self**	**Automatic** **Autonomy**

Prefixes	Meaning	Examples
Bene-	Good	Beneficial Benefactor
Bi- ; Bin-	Two	Bifocal Binoculars
Circu-	Around	Circulate Circumstances
Co-; Col-	Together	Coworker Collect
Contra-	Against	Contradiction Contrast
Counter-	Opposite	Counteraction Counterpart
Dis-	Lack of or negative	Disagreement Dishonesty
Ex-	Out or former	Exit Ex-husband
Fore-	Before	Foretell Foresee
Hyper-	Excessive	Hypertension Hypersensitive
Hypo-	Too little or beneath	Hypotension Hypodermic
Il-	Not	Illiterate Illegal
In-	Not	Incompatible Inevitable
Inter-	Among or between	Interference Interview
Ir-	Not	Irrelevant Irresponsibility

Prefixes	Meaning	Examples
Mal-	Bad or wrong	Maltreatment Malfunction
Mis-	Bad or wrong	Mistreat Misunderstand
Mono-	One	Monologue
Multi-	Many	Multinational Multicolored
Omni-	All	Omniscient Omnipotent
Over-	Too much	Overcrowded Overdose
Poly-	Many	Polytechnic Polyglot
Post-	After	Postgraduate Posthumous
Pre-	Before	Preview Predictable
Pro-	Before or in favor of	Pronoun Proficient
Re-	Again	Recollect Reflection
Syn-	With	Syndrome Synchronize
Trans-	Across	Transportation Transfer
Tri-	Three	Triangle Triceps
Un-	Not	Unnecessary Unavoidable
Under-	below	Undermine Underestimate

高頻率表示「否定」的字首整理

non-

肯定	否定
Violent 暴力	**Nonviolent** 非暴力
Stop 停止	**Nonstop** 不停
Sense 意義	**Nonsense** 無意義

un-

肯定	否定
Doubted 可疑的	**Undoubted** 無疑的
Common 共同的	**Uncommon** 不同的
Usual 平常的	**Unusual** 不平常的

in-

肯定	否定
Expensive 昂貴的	**Inexpensive** 不貴的
Complete 完整的	**Incomplete** 不完整的
Convenient 方便的	**Inconvenient** 不方便的

im-

肯定	否定
Possible可能的	**Impossible** 不可能的
Polite 禮貌的	**Impolite** 不禮貌的
Balance 平衡	**Imbalance** 不平衡

il-

肯定	否定
Legal 合法的	**Illegal** 不合法的
Legible可辨認的	**Illegible** 不可辨認的
Liberal自由的	**Illiberal** 拘泥的

ab-

肯定	否定
Normal 正常的	**Abnormal** 不正常的

ir-

肯定	否定
Resistible 可以抵抗的	**Irresistible** 無法抵抗的
Responsible 負責的	**Irresponsible** 不負責的
Rational 有理性的	**Irrational** 無理性的

dis-

肯定	否定
Cover 覆蓋	**Discover** 發覺
Agree 同意	**Disagree** 不同意
Like 喜歡	**Dislike** 不喜歡

mis-

肯定	否定
Understanding 了解	**Misunderstanding** 誤解
Apply 應用	**Misapply** 誤用
Arrange 安排	**Misarrange** 作錯誤的安排

高頻率常用的字根

Stems	Meaning	Examples
Bio	Life	Biology Biographer
Biblio	Book	Bibliography Bibliophile
Cycle	Circle	Recycle Tricycle
Demo	People	Democrat Democracy
Dict	Say	Contradict Predict
Dorm	Sleep	Dormant Dormitory
Duct	Lead	Conduct Deductive
Flect	Bend	Reflect Flexible
Graph	Writing	Autograph Photograph
Labor	Work	Laboratory Elaborate
Lingua	Language	Monolingual Bilingual
Temp	Time	Tempo Temperature
Vis	See	Vision Television

高頻率常用的字尾

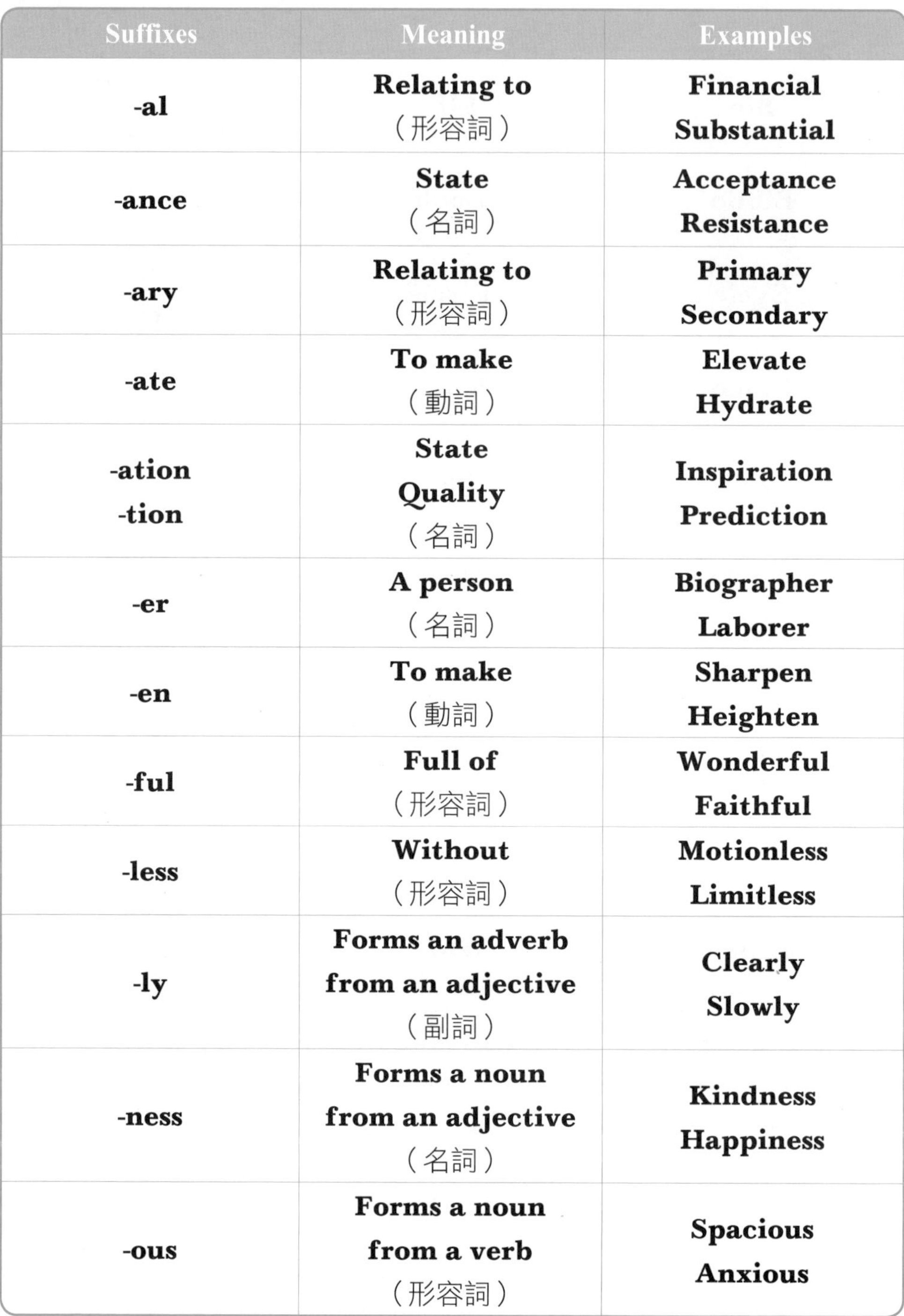

Suffixes	Meaning	Examples
-al	Relating to （形容詞）	Financial Substantial
-ance	State （名詞）	Acceptance Resistance
-ary	Relating to （形容詞）	Primary Secondary
-ate	To make （動詞）	Elevate Hydrate
-ation -tion	State Quality （名詞）	Inspiration Prediction
-er	A person （名詞）	Biographer Laborer
-en	To make （動詞）	Sharpen Heighten
-ful	Full of （形容詞）	Wonderful Faithful
-less	Without （形容詞）	Motionless Limitless
-ly	Forms an adverb from an adjective （副詞）	Clearly Slowly
-ness	Forms a noun from an adjective （名詞）	Kindness Happiness
-ous	Forms a noun from a verb （形容詞）	Spacious Anxious

高頻率表示「人」的字尾整理

-er

原形	人的字尾	中文意思
Compose	Composer	作曲者
Employ	Employer	雇主
Lecture	Lecturer	演説者
Manage	Manager	經理
Report	Reporter	記者

★例外：

原形	非「人」的意思	中文意思
Compute	Computer	電腦
Rule	Ruler	尺
Print	Printer	印表機

–or

原形	人的字尾	中文意思
Advise	Advisor	顧問
Audit	Auditor	稽核員
Conduct	Conductor	指揮
Edit	Editor	編輯
Operate	Operator	接線生

★例外：

原形	非「人」的意思	中文意思
Elevate	Elevator	電梯
Refrigerate	Refrigerator	冰箱
Escalate	Escalator	手扶梯

-ese

原形	人的字尾	中文意思
Japan	**Japanese**	日本人
Taiwan	**Taiwanese**	臺灣人
Vietnam	**Vietnamese**	越南人
Portugal	**Portuguese**	葡萄牙人

-an

原形	人的字尾	中文意思
America	**American**	美國人
Africa	**African**	非洲人
Russia	**Russian**	俄國人
Korea	**Korean**	韓國人

-ian

原形	人的字尾	中文意思
History	**Historian**	歷史學家
Music	**Musician**	音樂家
Physics	**Physician**	內科醫生
Politics	**Politician**	政治家

-ist

原形	人的字尾	中文意思
Art	**Artist**	藝術家
Novel	**Novelist**	小說家
Piano	**Pianist**	鋼琴家
Tour	**Tourist**	觀光客

-mate

原形	人的字尾	中文意思
Class	**Classmate**	同學
Room	**Roommate**	室友
Team	**Teammate**	隊友
Work	**Workmate**	同事

-ee

原形	人的字尾	中文意思
Address	**Addressee**	收信人
Commit	**Committee**	委員會成員
Employ	**Employee**	員工
Interview	**Interviewee**	面試者
Refuge	**Refugee**	難民
Train	**Trainee**	實習生

-eer

原形	人的字尾	中文意思
Engine	**Engineer**	工程師
Mountain	**Mountaineer**	登山者

-ess

原形	人的字尾	中文意思
Host	**Hostess**	女主人
Prince	**Princess**	公主
Steward	**Stewardess**	女空服員
Wait	**Waitress**	女服務生

Chapter 1 閱讀的字彙力

-ent

原形	人的字尾	中文意思
Oppose	**Opponent**	對手
Reside	**Resident**	居民

-ar

原形	人的字尾	中文意思
Beg	**Beggar**	乞丐
Lie	**Liar**	說謊者

-ster

原形	人的字尾	中文意思
Mini	**Minister**	部長
Gang	**Gangster**	歹徒
Spin	**Spinster**	老女人
Young	**Youngster**	年輕人

-ant

原形	人的字尾	中文意思
Account	**Accountant**	會計
Assist	**Assistant**	助理
Occupy	**Occupant**	居民
Serve	**Servant**	服務生

字的聯想：同義與反義、形似易混淆、多重涵義

了解一般常用的字首、字根與字尾後，另一種學習單字的方式是，盡量整理與延伸所有認識的單字，也就是說，當我們了解一個單字之後，就要再了解它的同義反義字或是形似與易混淆的字彙，亦或是多重涵義的字彙。

字彙整理

常用同義字

1. allow = permit 允許
2. ban = forbid 禁止
3. aid = help = assistant 協助
4. astonishment = surprise = shock 吃驚
5. beverages = drinks 飲料
6. empty = blank = vacant 空的
7. bright = shinning 明亮
8. broad = wide 寬廣的
9. reason = cause 原因
10. careful = cautious 小心的
11. choice = selection = option = alternative 選擇
12. constant= frequent = continuous 持續的
13. dangerous = risky 危險
14. decrease = reduce 減少
15. demonstration = display = show = exhibition 展示
16. disease = sickness = illness 生病
17. earn = gain 獲得
18. energetic = active 精力旺盛
19. entire = whole 整個

20. fashionable = stylish 流行的
21. gather = collect 收集
22. general = common = usual 一般的
23. glance = take a look at 看一眼
24. inquire = ask 詢問
25. portion = part = segment = fraction 部分
26. purchase = buy 購買
27. prompt =quick 迅速
28. intention = purpose 目的
29. spread = scatter 散布
30. suitable = appropriate 適當的
31. trust = believe 相信

常用反義字

1. absent – present（缺席－出席）
2. accept – refuse（接受－婉拒）
3. amateur – professional（業餘－專業）
4. attack – defend（攻擊－防禦）
5. artificial – genuine（人工的－自然的）
6. broad – narrow（寬的－窄的）
7. clever – foolish（聰明的－愚蠢的）
8. construct – destroy（建造－毀滅）
9. shallow – deep（淺的－深的）
10. empty – full（空的－滿的）
11. exit – entrance（出口－入口）
12. failure – success（失敗－成功）
13. familiar – strange（熟悉－陌生）
14. forbid – permit（禁止－允許）

15. find – lose（發現－遺失）

16. fresh – stale（新鮮的－腐壞的）

17. host – guest（主人－客人）

18. generous – selfish（慷慨的－自私的）

19. nice – mean（好的－凶惡的）

20. outgoing – shy（外向的－內向的）

21. open-minded – narrow-minded（心胸寬大的－心胸狹窄的）

22. negative – positive（負面的－正面的）

23. public – private（公共的－私有的）

24. permanent – temporary（永久的－暫時的）

25. pleasure – pain（愉快的－痛苦的）

26. safe – dangerous（安全的－危險的）

27. victory – defeat（勝利－挫敗）

28. appear – disappear（出現－消失）

29. common – uncommon（平常的－不平常的）

30. ordinary – extraordinary（一般的－不平凡的）

31. convenient – inconvenient（方便的－不方便的）

32. polite – impolite（禮貌的－不禮貌的）

33. normal – abnormal（正常的－不正常的）

34. bright – dark（光明的－黑暗的）

35. fixed – flexible（固定的－彈性的）

常用有關人個性描寫的形容詞與其反義字

中文	英文	中文（反義）	英文（反義）
認真的	**Hardworking**	懶惰的	**Lazy**
大方的	**Generous**	小氣的	**Stingy**
活潑的	**Outgoing**	害羞的	**Shy**
心胸寬大的	**Open-minded**	心胸狹窄的	**Narrow-minded**

中文	英文	中文（反義）	英文（反義）
溫柔的	**Gentle**	粗暴的	**Rough**
有魅力的	**Charming**	無聊的	**Boring**
有趣的	**Interesting**	無趣的	**Dull**
仔細的	**Careful**	粗心的	**Careless**
有活力的	**Energetic**	無精打采的	**Listless**
勇敢的	**Brave**	膽小的	**Timid**
有耐心的	**Patient**	無耐心的	**Impatient**
成熟的	**Mature**	幼稚的	**Childish**
有責任的	**Responsible**	不負責的	**Irresponble**
誠實的	**Honest**	不誠實的	**Dishonest**
體貼的	**Considerate**	不體貼的	**Inconsiderate**
老練的	**Sophisticated**	單純的	**Simple**
有教育的	**Educated**	未受教育的	**Uneducated**
優雅的	**Graceful**	笨手笨腳的	**Clumsy**
冷靜的	**Calm**	激動的	**Excited**
慈祥的	**Kind**	邪惡的	**Mean**
隨和的	**Easygoing**	嚴格的	**Strict**
有彈性的	**Flexible**	固執的	**Stubborn**
主動的	**Active**	被動的	**Passive**
新潮的	**Trendy**	過時的	**Old-fashioned**
安靜的	**Quiet**	多話的	**Talkative**

閱讀常見之字形相似易混淆字彙

1. abroad 海外 / aboard 登上
2. accept 接受 / except 除此之外
3. adapt適應 / adopt 採取
4. affect 影響 / effect 效果
5. affective 情感的 / effective 有效的

6. announce 宣布 / pronounce 發音
7. assign 指派 / design 設計 / resign 辭職
8. attach 附加 / attack 攻擊
9. beside 旁邊 / besides 此外
10. carton 紙箱 / cartoon 卡通
11. command 命令 / comment 評論
12. complement 補充 / compliment 恭維
13. dessert 甜點 / desert 沙漠
14. despise 瞧不起 / despite 儘管
15. disinterested 公正的 / uninterested 無興趣的
16. distinctive 獨特的 / distinct 明顯的
17. explode 爆炸 / explore 探索
18. heel 腳跟 / heal 治療
19. imaginary 虛構的 / imaginative 有想像力的
20. immoral 不道德的 / immortal 不朽的
21. lie 平躺；說謊 / lay 放置；下蛋
22. lighten 變輕 / lightning 閃電
23. loyal 忠誠的 / royal 皇室的
24. personal 個人的 / personnel 人事的
25. plan 計畫 / plane 飛機 / plain 平原
26. principal 校長 / principle 原則
27. propose 提議 / purpose 目的
28. prescribe 開藥 / subscribe 訂閱
29. quiet 安靜 / quite 相當地
30. raise 舉起 / rise 升起
31. refer 提及 / infer 推斷
32. reject 反對 / inject 注射
33. receipt 收據 / recipe 食譜
34. stationary 固定不動的 / stationery 文具
35. towel 毛巾 / tower 塔台
36. vacation 假期 / vocation 職業

練習題 寫出正確的字 EXERCISES

1. aboard / abroad

   (1) He had gone ________ on business.

   (2) They went ________ the ship.

2. access / assess

   (1) Students need easy ________ to books in the library.

   (2) They ________ the house at $1000,000.

3. beside / besides

   (1) There are a lot of people at the party ________ us.

   (2) I am sitting ________ my friend, Charles.

4. confident / confidential

   (1) The ________ agreement should be signed soon.

   (2) I am ________ in winning the first place.

5. desert / dessert

   (1) What would you like for your ________?

   (2) He ________ his family and left for the USA.

   (3) The land without water is a ________.

6. loose / lose

   (1) Can I have a ________ pair of pants?

   (2) Please do not ________ your concert ticket.

7. hospital / hospitality

   (1) Thanks for your ________ during the visit.

   (2) The injured were sent to the ________ soon.

解答

1. aboard / abroad

   (1) He had gone abroad（出國）on business.

   (2) They went aboard（登上）the ship.

2. access / assess

   (1) Students need easy access（接近使用）to books in the library.

   (2) They assess（評估）the house at $1000,000.

3. beside / besides

   (1) There are a lot of people at the party besides（除……之外）us.

   (2) I am sitting beside（在旁邊）my friend, Charles.

4. confident / confidential

   (1) The confidential（機密的） agreement should be signed soon.

   (2) I am confident（有自信的） in winning the first place.

5. desert / dessert

   (1) What would you like for your desserts（甜點）?

   (2) He deserted（拋棄） his family and left for the USA.

   (3) The land without water is a desert（沙漠）.

6. loose / lose

   (1) Can I have a loose（鬆垮） pair of pants?

   (2) Please do not lose（遺失） your concert ticket.

7. hospital / hospitality

   (1) Thanks for your hospitality（好客款待） during the visit.

   (2) The injured were sent to the hospital（醫院） soon.

字彙整理

閱讀常見之同源形容詞

Sensible 明智的	**Sensitive** 敏感的
Continual 斷斷續續的	**Continuous** 連續不斷的
Intense 強烈的	**Intensive** 精深的
Respectable 值得尊敬的	**Respective** 各別的
Imaginable 可以想像的	**Imaginative** 有想像力的
Intelligent 有才智的	**Intelligible** 易領悟的
Alternate 輪流的	**Alternative** 選擇的
Politic 精明的	**Political** 政治的
Beneficial 有益的	**Beneficent** 多多行善的
Credible 可靠的	**Creditable** 可稱讚的
Regretful 遺憾的（人）	**Regrettable** 遺憾的（事物）
Seasonable 及時的	**Seasonal** 季節的
Likely 可能的	**Likable** 可愛的
Elementary 基礎的	**Elemental** 自然的
Official 官方的	**Officious** 多管閒事的
Confident 有自信的	**Confidential** 機密的
Memorable 值得記憶的	**Memorial** 紀念的
Social 社會的	**Sociable** 社交的
Childish 幼稚的	**Childlike** 孩子般的
Distinct 明顯的	**Distinctive** 獨特的
Classic 經典的	**Classical** 古典的
Comprehensible 可以理解的	**Comprehensive** 全面的
Disinterested 公平的	**Uninterested** 沒興趣的
Effective 有效的	**Efficient** 有效率的
Fleshly 肉體的	**Fleshy** 肥胖的

Historic 歷史上著名的	**Historical** 歷史上的
Electric 有電的；用電的	**Electronic** 電子的
Economic 經濟的	**Economical** 節約的
Industrial 工業的	**Industrious** 勤勉的
Considerate 體貼的	**Considerable** 相當大量的
Impractical 不切合實際的	**Impracticable** 無法使用的
Mysterious 神祕的	**Mystical** 奧妙的
Notable 著名的（人）	**Noted** 著名的（事物）

常用多重涵義字

1. **appear**
   - As soon as the shower passed, a rainbow appeared in the sky. 出現(v.)
   - He appears to be unhappy. 似乎(v.)
2. **book**
   - Put those books on the shelf. 書(n.)
   - Our hotel is fully booked. 預訂(v.)
3. **bright**
   - Always look at the bright side. 明亮的(adj.)
   - She is a bright girl. 聰明的(adj.)
4. **change**
   - I need to change my diet. 改變(v.)
   - Here is your change, $2.07 零錢(n.)
5. **class**
   - The class are reading aloud. 學生(n.)
   - I always take a yoga class after work. 課程(n.)
6. **company**
   - ACME is a foreign company. 公司(n.)
   - She is always my company when I need her. 同伴(n.)

7. **check**

- All passengers need to check their luggage. 檢查(v.)
- I'd like to pay my tuition by check. 支票(n.)

8. **date**

- What is the date today? 日期(n.)
- She is my date. 約會（的對象）(n.)

9. **fix**

- A repairman is fixing the light. 修理(v.)
- My mother has already fixed the dinner. 準備(v.)

10. **fair**

- The trade fair is well-attended. 展覽會(n.)
- It is fair today. There is not a cloud in the sky. 晴朗的(adj.)

11. **left**

- At last, we left without saying goodbye. 離開(v.)
- If you turn to the left, you will find our house. 左邊(n.)

12. **lie**

- Don't tell a lie. 說謊(n.)
- Lie on the back. 平躺(v.)

13. **light**

- The tennis racket is light. 輕的(adj.)
- Turn on the light. It's dark inside. 燈(n.)

14. **match**

- Never play with a match. 火柴(n.)
- The tennis match took place yesterday. 比賽(n.)

15. **mean**

- I didn't mean it. 意指(v.)
- The dog is so mean. 凶惡(adj.)

16. **note**

- I lost my notes from the meeting. 紀錄(n.)
- This is a ten-pound note. 紙鈔(n.)

17. **train**

- The swimmers are in training. 訓練(n.)
- The train is coming up quickly. 火車(n.)

18. **plant**

- The gardener is planting flowers in the garden. 種植(v.)
- The company has some plants overseas. 工廠(n.)

19. **rest**

- I am exhausted. I need some rest. 休息(n.)
- Are you sure he is the man that you want to live for the rest of your life? 剩餘(n.)

20. **address**

- Give him your address. 地址(n.)
- She is addressing the group. 演說(v.)

21. **meet**

- We meet every weekend. 遇見(v.)
- They are running in the meet. 運動會(n.)

22. **minute**

- Wait a minute. 分鐘(n.)
- I need the board minutes. 會議紀錄(n.)

23. **fine**

- My parents are fine. 很好的(adj.)
- The fine will be imposed soon. 罰款(n.)

24. **kind**

- It’s very kind of you to say that. 仁慈的(adj.)
- What kind of movies do you like? 種類(n.)

25. **plain**

- I want to order a plain pizza. 普通的(adj.)
- Beyond the plain is a high hill. 平原(n.)

26. **fall**

- Do not fall off the bike. 掉落(v.)
- I like the weather in fall. 秋天(n.)

27. **contract**

- The two words are contracted. 縮寫(v.)
- We have to sign this contract. 合約(n.)

28. **live**

- I live in the suburb. 住(v.)
- The live whale is interesting. 活的(adj.)

29. **record**

- He holds the record in the high jump. 紀錄(n.)
- They want to record Charles's class. 錄音(v.)

30. **export**

- He is in the export business. 出口(n.)
- The oranges are exported. 出口(v.)

31. **desert**

- The land without water is a desert. 沙漠(n.)
- You are deserted. 遺棄 (v.)

32. **present**

- He was present in the meeting in the end. 出席(adj.)
- I get a birthday present every year. 禮物(n)

33. **progress**

- They progress in their studies. 進步(v.)
- They made progress. 進展(n.)

34. **tear**

- She was moved to <u>tears</u>. 眼淚(n.)
- They try to <u>tear</u> down the building. 拆除(v.)

35. **contest**

- A speech <u>contest</u> will take place soon. 比賽(n.)
- He wants to <u>contest</u> with me. 比賽(v.)

36. **object**

- We <u>objected</u> to this plan. 反對(v.)
- The <u>object</u> is really an eyesore. 物體(n.)

容易混淆的字組四十組

1. **assent** n. 同意

- His parents gave assent to his plan to study abroad.
  （他的父母同意他出國念書的計畫。）

ascent n. 提升

- His ascent as a manager was the result of his hard work.
  （他由於工作認真而晉升為經理。）

2. **assay** v. 嘗試

- Let's assay the western part of the city first.
  （讓我們先試著到這城市的西部看看。）

essay v. 嘗試

- She essayed her own opinion in her university term paper.
  （她嘗試在學期報告中發表她的意見。）

3. **attend to** 注意；照顧

- Attend to the baby so he doesn't get hurt or lost.
  （注意小嬰兒不要讓他受傷或走失。）

tend to 有某種傾向

- People who eat a lot of fatty foods tend to be overweight.
  （吃太多油炸食物的人均傾向肥胖。）

4. **aisle** n. 走道

- Don't block the aisle of the plane with your luggage.
  （不要把行李擋在飛機走道上。）

isle n. 島嶼

- I want to live on an isle in the Pacific where I won't have too many neighbors.
  （我想住在太平洋裡一個沒有很多鄰居的島上。）

5. **allusion** n. 提及；引述

- I only made an allusion to my roommate's dirty clothes without saying anything too directly.
  （我只提到我室友的一些髒衣服，而沒把話說得太直。）

illusion n. 錯覺

- The magician performed many amazing illusions.
  （魔術師表演許多令人驚豔的錯覺。）

6. **adapt** v. 使適應

- You must have the ability to adapt if you want to live in a foreign country.
  （假如你要住在國外就必須要有適應能力。）

adopt v. 採用；領養

- My friend, who is unable to make a baby of her own, has decided to adopt a child.
  （我的一個無法生育的朋友決定要領養一個小孩。）

adept adj. 熟練的

- She was adept at cooking and always made delicious meals.
  （她熟練煮飯所以總是可以煮出美食。）

7. **addition** n. 附加
   - The addition of sugar makes the cereal taste good.
     （加了糖使麥片變得可口。）

   edition n. 版本；版
   - I always buy the morning edition of the newspaper on my way to work.
     （我在上班的途中買了份早報。）

8. **affect** v. 影響
   - Diet will affect your health.
     （節食影響健康。）

   effect n. 影響
   - Poor health is the effect of eating too much junk food.
     （吃太多垃圾食物將影響健康。）

9. **anarchy** n. 無政府狀態；混亂
   - When the elections failed to produce a majority leader, anarchy occurred.
     （當選舉結果無法產生一個多數領袖時，無政府狀態就發生了。）

   architect n. 建築師
   - The government hired an architect to design a new city hall building.
     （政府雇用了一個建築師來設計一個新的市政大樓。）

10. **astrology** n. 占星術
    - He really believes in astrology and never goes out before reading about his star sign in the newspaper.
      （他十分相信占星術且在他出門前一定會閱讀報紙的星座運勢。）

    astronomy n. 天文學
    - He was interested in planets and stars so he studied astronomy.
      （他對行星和星星有興趣所以研讀天文學。）

11. **audible** adj. 可聽見的

- In the library, your voice must not be audible to the other people looking at books.
  （在圖書館中，你的聲音不可以吵到其他正在看書的人。）

audience n. 聽眾；觀眾

- The audience clapped when the movies was over.
  （當電影結束時，觀眾都鼓掌。）

12. **audit** n. 查帳

- The government had some questions about his earnings so they audited his tax return.
  （政府對他的收入有疑問，因此他們查他的稅。）

audition n. 試演

- Actors must perform at an audition to earn a part in a play.
  （演員必須在舞台上試演一段以贏得一個劇本裡的角色。）

13. **auditor** n. 聽者；旁聽生；查帳員

- The auditor needed to see all the receipts and my previous tax return.
  （查帳者需要看所有的收據以及我先前的繳稅單。）

auditorium n. 禮堂；觀眾席

- Everyone sat in the auditorium to listen to the concert.
  （所有人坐在禮堂聽音樂會。）

14. **caption** n. 標題

- The caption explained what happened in the picture.
  （這標題解釋著這圖片發生的事。）

captious adj. 詭辯的；吹毛求疵的

- I didn't enjoy talking to him because his captious nature always made me feel nervous.
  （我不喜歡和他說話，因為他詭辯的個性總是令我覺得緊張。）

captivate vt. 使迷惑

- She didn't move for the entire concert because she was captivated by the singer's voice.
  （她在整場的音樂會中一動也不動，因為她被歌手的聲音完全迷住了。）

15. **capture** v. 捉

- The spider captures a fly in its web.
  （蜘蛛在牠的網內抓到一隻蒼蠅。）

captain n. 船長

- The ship's captain ordered the crew to return to the harbor when the weather became too rough.
  （當氣候變得十分惡劣時，船長命令他的船員回港。）

16. **recession** n. 撤回、衰退

- There are fewer new jobs when the economy is in a recession.
  （在衰退的經濟中工作機會則愈少。）

secession n. 脫離；退出

- The rest of the United Nations membership worried that the secession of a few countries would weaken the power of the organization.
  （剩餘的聯合國會員擔心一些退出的國家將削弱這組織的實力。）

17. **secede** vi. 脫離；退出

- A group of poor countries was unhappy with decisions being made at the United Nations and decided to secede.
  （一些較窮的國家因為不滿聯合國的決議而退出。）

decide vt. 決定

- He decided to eat at the restaurant right in front of him, so he walked in.
  （他決定去吃他對面的那家餐廳，因此他走進去了。）

18. **homicide** n. 殺人者

- She killed her boss and was charged with the crime of homicide.
（她殺了她的老闆，因而被控殺人罪。）

suicide n. 自殺

- The businessman lost all his money and was so depressed that he committed suicide by jumping off a bridge.
（這個生意人失去了所有的錢而十分沮喪，因此他跳橋自殺。）

19. **cosmetic** n. 化妝品

- She looked in the mirror to apply her lipstick and other cosmetics.
（她看著鏡子擦口紅和化妝。）

cosmic adj. 宇宙的

- Astronauts are interested in all cosmic things , such as planets and stars.
（太空人對宇宙的事物如行星和星星有興趣。）

20. **sccurate** adj. 正確的

- She spoke accurate English and never made a grammar mistake.
（她能說出正確的英文並且從未犯文法的錯誤。）

cure vt. , vi. 治療；治癒

- People go to the doctors to cure their illnesses.
（人們去看醫生治療他們的疾病。）

21. **manicure** n. 修指甲

- She went to a beauty salon for a manicure because she liked to have well cared for hands.
（她想去美容院修她的指甲是因為她喜歡讓她的雙手得到良好的照顧。）

secure adj. 無慮的；安全的

- This is a secure hiding place.
（這是一個安全的藏匿所。）

22. **accede** v. 同意

- We shall accede to your request for more evidence.

  （如果有更充分的證據，我們會同意你的請求。）

concede v. 勉強承認

- To avoid delay, we shall concede that more evidence is necessary.

  （為了避免延誤，我們不得不承認需要更充分的證據。）

exceed v. 超過 **(= to be more than)**

- Some of the autos exceed the speed-limit.

  （有些汽車超過速率限制。）

23. **access** n. 接近、進入或使用（人、地或物）之權

- Professors have free access to the library.

  （教授可以自由使用圖書館。）

excess n. 過度；過分

- Don't carry your grief to excess.

  （不要過度悲傷。）

24. **accept** v. 接受

- He accepted a present from his friend.

  （他接受了朋友的禮物。）

except prep. 除……之外

- We all went except Tom.

  （除湯姆外，我們都去了。）

25. **breath** n. 呼吸

- Before you dive in, take a very deep breath.

  （你在潛水前，先做個深呼吸。）

breathe v. 呼吸

- It is difficult to breathe under water.

  （在水面下呼吸很困難。）

breadth n. 寬度

- In a square, the breadth should be equal to the length.

（正方形的寬要與長相等。）

26. **coarse** adj. 粗俗的

- Don't use coarse words before a lady.

（不要在女士面前講粗話。）

course n. 課程

- Which course in English are you taking?

（你選修哪個英文課程?）

27. **comic** adj. 喜劇的

- A clown is a comic figure.

（小丑是個喜劇人物。）

comical adj. 滑稽的

- The peculiar hat she wore gave her a comical appearance.

（她戴的那頂奇怪帽子，使她的外表看起來很滑稽。）

28. **conscience** n. 良心

- Man's conscience prevents him from becoming completely selfish.

（良心使人類免於完全的自私。）

conscientious adj. 忠心的；正直的

- We all depend on him because he is conscientious.

（由於他很忠心，所以我們都仰賴他。）

conscious adj. 知道的；有意的

- The injured man was completely conscious.

（這名受傷的人非常清醒。）

29. **compare to** 比喻

- A minister is sometimes compared to a shepherd.

（牧師有時被比喻為牧羊人。）

compared with 比較

- Shakespeare's plays are often compared with those of Marlowe.
  （莎士比亞的劇作常被拿來與馬羅的劇作比較。）

contrast with 對比

- Contrast these foreign goods with the domestic products.
  （將這些外國貨和本國貨對比。）

30. **complement** n. 補充物

- Love is the complement of the law.
  （愛是法律的補充物=法律中需要有愛的精神，才算完備。）

compliment n. 稱讚

- A sincere compliment boost's one's morale.
  （由衷的稱讚可鼓舞一個人的精神。）

31. **council** n. 會議

- The City Council enacts local laws and regulations.
  （市議會通過了地方法律和規定。）

counsel n. 勸告

- He gave me good counsel on this matter.
  （對於這件事，他給我很好的忠告。）

32. **descent** n. 降下

- The descent into the cave was treacherous.
  （下到這個洞穴的路很危險。）

dissent n. 不同意

- He expressed the strong dissent when his friend suggested this plan.
  （當他的朋友建議這個計畫時，他表現強烈的異議。）

33. **desert** n. 沙漠

- The Sahara is the most famous desert in the world.
  （撒哈拉是世界上最有名的沙漠。）

desert v. 拋棄

- A husband must not desert his wife.
（丈夫不可拋棄妻子。）

dessert n. 餐後甜點

- After lunch，we had pudding for dessert.
（吃過午餐之後，我們吃布丁作為餐後甜點。）

34. **dual** adj. 二的；二重的

- Dr. White had a dual personality.
（懷特博士有雙重性格。）

duel n. 決鬥

- John was fatally injured in a duel with Tom.
（約翰在和湯姆的決鬥中，受了致命傷。）

35. **emerge** v. 出現

- The swimmer emerged from the pool.
（這個游泳的人從泳池裡出來。）

immerge v. 浸入

- Test the temperature before immerging yourself in the pool.
（浸入游泳池之前，先試一試溫度。）

36. **emigrate** v. 自本國遷居到他國

- The Norwegians emigrated to America in the mid-1860's.
（挪威人於一八六〇年中，移民到美國。）

immigrate v. 自外國移來

- Many Norwegians immigrant into the Middle West of the USA.
（許多挪威人移民進美國中西部。）

37. **persecute** v. 迫害

- Christians were terribly persecuted.
（基督徒受到嚴重迫害。）

prosecute v. 實行

- He prosecuted an inquiry into reasons for the company's failure.
  （他調查了公司倒閉的原因。）

38. **proceed** v. 繼續進行

- Proceed with what you were doing.
  （繼續做你原來在做的事。）

supersede v. 替代

- It is then possible that Plan B will supersede Plan A.
  （那麼 B 計畫將可能取代 A 計畫。）

39. **principal** adj. 主要的

- Taipei is the principal city of Taiwan.
  （臺北是臺灣首要的城市。）

principle n. 原則

- This is a basic principle.
  （這是基本原則。）

40. **stationary** adj. 固定的

- A factory engine is stationary.
  （工廠的發動機是固定的。）

stationery n. 文具

- We bought writing paper at the stationery store.
  （我們在文具店買寫信用的紙。）

1.3 字的聯想：同形結尾或開頭的字

還有一種單字的記憶方式是把同形開頭或是同形結尾的字整理在一起來作單字的記憶，這一類的整理也多為應付各類英文考試的最佳利器。

-pire

Expire 滿期，屆期；（期限）終止

Conspire 同謀，密謀

Respire 呼吸

Aspire 熱望，嚮往；懷有大志

Inspire 鼓舞，激勵，驅使

Perspire 出汗，流汗；辛勞，苦幹

-volve

Evolve 逐步形成；發展；進化；成長

Devolve 被轉移，被移交

Involve 使捲入，連累；牽涉

Revolve 旋轉，自轉

-rupt

Bankrupt 破產的；有關破產的

Interrupt 打斷（講話或講話人）

Abrupt 突然的；意外的

Erupt 噴出；爆發

Corrupt 腐敗的，貪污的

-scribe

Describe 描寫，描繪，敘述

Prescribe 開（藥方），為……開（藥方）；囑咐

Subscribe 訂閱；訂購（書籍等）

Conscribe 徵召……入伍

Circumscribe 在周圍畫線；限制

-serve

Observe 看到，注意到

Reserve 儲備，保存；保留

Deserve 應受

Preserve 保存，保藏；防腐

Conserve 保存；保護；節省

-mit

Admit 承認

Commit 犯（罪），做（錯事等）

Emit 散發，放射；發出

Limit 限制；限定

Omit 遺漏；省略；刪去

Permit 允許，許可，准許

Remit 傳送；匯寄

Submit 提交，呈遞

Transmit 傳送，傳達

Vomit 嘔吐

-ficient

Efficient 效率高的；有能力的，能勝任的

Sufficient 足夠的，充分的

Deficient 不足的，缺乏的

Proficient 精通的，熟練的

-merge

Emerge 浮現；出現

Submerge 把……浸入水中，淹沒

Merge 使（公司等）合併

-dict

Predict 預言；預料；預報

Contradict 否定（陳述等）；反駁；提出論據反對

Indict 控告，告發；（尤指大陪審團）對……起訴

Interdict 禁止；制止

-ply

Reply 回答，答覆

Imply 暗指；暗示；意味著

Supply 供給，供應，提供

Apply 申請，請求

Comply（對要求、命令等）依從，順從，遵從

-vise

Advise 勸告，忠告

Devise 設計；發明；策劃；想出

Revise 修訂；校訂

Up-

Upbeat 令人樂觀的；歡快的

Upcoming 即將來臨的

Update 更新

Upfront 直率的；坦白的

Upgrade 使升級；提高；提升

Uphold 維護；維持；贊成；確認

Upholstery 室內裝潢品；（沙發等的）墊襯物；室內裝潢業

Out-

Outfit（尤指在特殊場合穿的）全套服裝

Outdated 過時的

Outdo 勝過；超越

Outgoing 外出的；出發的；即將離職的

Outgrowth 自然的發展；後果

Outing 遠足；郊遊；短途旅遊

Outlandish 異國風格的；古怪的

Outlaw 歹徒，罪犯，亡命之徒

Outlay 費用（額）

1.4 一般英文書信或商業廣告中常見的縮寫義涵

另外，別忘了英文的閱讀中，我們常會見到一些所謂「縮寫」的代表字，這種情形常出現在一般的商用書信或者是商業廣告中，能多了解一些這些縮寫字的意思，對於我們的閱讀理解，也會有絕對的幫助。

字彙整理

閱讀常見之英文書信縮寫義涵

1. ASAP (= as soon as possible) 儘快
2. BRB (= be right back) 馬上回來
3. BTW (= by the way) 對了
4. BFN (= bye for now) 再見
5. EZ (= easy) 容易
6. FYI (= for your information) 給你參考
7. FWIW (= for what it's worth) 確實有它的價值
8. HHOK (= ha ha only kidding) 哈哈！開玩笑的
9. HTH (= hope this helps) 希望這能夠幫得上忙
10. IMO (= in my opinion) 依我來看
11. IMHO (= in my humble opinion) 依我的淺見
12. IOW (= in other words) 換句話說

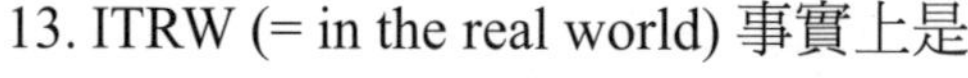

13. ITRW (= in the real world) 事實上是
14. LOL (= laughing out loud) 大笑
15. OIC (= on, I see) 我了解了
16. OTOH (= on the other hand) 另一方面
17. PLS (= please) 請
18. POC (= piece of cake) 小事一件
19. POV (= point of view) 觀點
20. TIA (= thanks in advance) 先謝了
21. TKS (= thanks) 謝謝
22. TTYL (= talk to you later) 晚點再聊
23. WRT (= with regards to) 關於……

閱讀常見之商業廣告縮寫義涵

1. w / = with = 帶有……
2. apt. = apartment =公寓
3. a / c = air conditioning = 冷氣設備
4. avail. = available = 可獲得的
5. Conv. = convenient = 方便的
6. elec. = electricity = 電力
7. Fpl. = fireplace = 壁爐
8. incl. = including = 包含
9. Kit. = kitchen = 廚房
10. Loc.= location = 位置
11. mod. = modern = 現代化的
12. trans. = transportation = 交通運輸
13. utils. = utility = 公共設施

Chapter 2

閱讀的理解力

一般閱讀的惡習有：逐字逐句的唸出聲或是每次只唸個別字，亦或是不斷重複看讀上文；這樣的閱讀方式不但速度慢，也難理解文中的含義。其實，在閱讀文章時，我們應該做到先找出文章的主旨與重點以及作者的立場（這個部分通常是在文中的主題句或是結論句可以找出）。同時，我們在閱讀時，要用手當作游標，一句一句的往下讀，遇到單字勿中斷，更不要立即地查閱字典，要會先作字彙的猜測。若是為了英文閱讀的考試，別忘了要先過目一下問題，了解之後再閱讀文章需要注意的內容。如問 “who” 時，在讀文章時就要特別注意人名或是職業別；若是問 “when” 則要特別注意日期或時間，或是 “before”，“after”，“by the time” 等連接詞；若是問 “why” 就要特別注意因果關係句，或是 “because”，“since”，“due to”，“as a result of” 等連接詞與介系詞。

一般文章中，若是出現所謂的「生字」時，我們可以做以下的處理。例如：

(1) The report's information comes from some famous biometerorologists. These well-known scientists are doing some about weather researches.

說明 我們通常可以從後一句的解釋來推測先前一句的單字，所以本句中的「biometerorologists」其實也就是「weather researchers」的意思。

(2) The man just carried the little boy into a van in a very short time. We were all very shocked and couldn't say a word about the kidnapping. That's horrible.

說明 我們也可以從前一句的說明來了解後一句中的單字意思，所以本句中的「kidnapping」，可以由「The man just carried the little boy into a van in a very short time」來解釋「綁架」的意思。

(3) Pests may cause serious famine, for instance, ants and rats attacked Indonesia's crops in 1566 and 1568 respectively, and these causes over 1 million residents had no food to eat at these times.

說明 我們也可以從for example, for instance, in other words, that is, that is to say, such as等轉折詞 (transitions) 來了解前述的單字意思，所以本句中的「pests」，可以由「for instance, ants and rats」來解釋為「害蟲」的意思。

平時閱讀時也可以練習試著問自己問題，考試時即可在讀問題前先預測到可能會被問的問題。基本上常會有下列 7 類問題：

1. 主旨大意題：問文章的主旨、大意或適合的標題，例如「What is a good title for this story?」或「What is the best title for this article?」
2. 細部資訊題：問文章內重要的細部資訊，例如「Where do Amy and her family live?」或「When will the students have to hand in their reports?」或「What of the following statements is NOT true?」
3. 推測場景及理解文章脈絡題：問可能讀到該文的場合，例如「Where might a person see this?」或「Where can people see this?」
4. 闡釋 / 推論題：問作者未於文中直接寫出之訊息、言外之意，考應用所得資訊進行推論，例如「What else must you tell the waiter?」或「What

does this report imply?」

5. 詢問閱讀的對象：例如「Who is likely to respond to this ad?」或「Who is this notice mainly written to?」
6. 數學算術題：問文章內的數字資訊，例如「According to the notice, if Helen buys the meal, how much does she owe?」
7. 解釋文章中的單字或片語題：例如「The word "organic" in line 5 means?」或「The phrase "catch up" can be replaced by?」

2.1 閱讀力的提升：找主題與主旨Finding the topic and main idea

在閱讀時，我們需先看一下整篇文章與高頻率重複的字組，這些相同或是類似的字組，就是我們所謂的「關鍵字」(key words)。而抓住這些關鍵字的動作，就稱作「掃描」(scanning)。掃描是我們在做閱讀時一項重要的工作。經由掃描所獲得的關鍵字，往往讓讀者對於一篇文章的重點能先窺知一二。例如：

(1) Arabic / English / Japanese / Chinese 代表 languages
(2) dogs / cats / fish / turtles 代表 pets
(3) spring / summer / fall / winter 代表 seasons
(4) tennis / bowling / hockey / badminton 代表 sports
(5) sofa / desk / rug / bookcase 代表 furniture
(6) May / June / September / December 代表 months
(7) living room / dining room / bedroom / bathroom 代表 rooms
(8) Charles / Jessica / Bill / Will 代表 names
(9) telephone / email / fax / text messages 代表 ways to communicate
(10) flute / violin / piano / guitar 代表 musical instruments

MAIN IDEA（主旨）

Favorite foods	Toys
Summer	Television
School	Farm
Christmas	Store

1. The Main Idea:____________________________
   cartoons on Saturday / movies / my favorite show
2. The Main Idea:____________________________
   pizza / French fries / hamburgers
3. The Main Idea:____________________________
   trains / squirt guns / balls
4. The Main Idea:____________________________
   swimming / vacation / no school
5. The Main Idea:____________________________
   money / customers / clothes
6. The Main Idea:____________________________
   Santa Claus / gifts / tree
7. The Main Idea:____________________________
   animals / barn / crops
8. The Main Idea:____________________________
   teacher / desks / pencils

MAIN IDEA（主旨）

Favorite foods	Toys
Summer	Television
School	Farm
Christmas	Store

1. The Main Idea:

   Television: cartoons on Saturday / movies / my favorite show

2. The Main Idea:

   Favorite foods: pizza / French fries / hamburgers

3. The Main Idea:

   Toys: trains / squirt guns / balls

4. The Main Idea:

   Summer: swimming / vacation / no school

5. The Main Idea:

   Store: money / customers / clothes

6. The Main Idea:

   Christmas: Santa Claus / gifts / tree

7. The Main Idea:

   Farm: animals / barn / crops

8. The Main Idea:

   School: teacher / desks / pencils

2.2 閱讀力的提升：找主題句與結論句 Finding the topic sentence and concluding sentence

找出一篇文章的主題句與結論句，往往代表一篇文章的主旨與大意，了解主題句與結論句有助於了解文章要探討的重點與其作者的立場。

例一

Last Sunday, Mr. and Mrs. Wang went to a steakhouse to celebrate their 20th wedding anniversary. While they were enjoying their meal, the fire alarm went off; then they saw the flames coming out of the kitchen. Mr. and Mrs. Wang rushed down the stairs to escape from this terrible fire. Soon, the fire engines arrived. A short time later, the fire was under control and everything was fine. It is an unforgettable day for Mr. and Mrs. Wang and they will never forget it.

✻ 主題句：敘述去餐廳慶祝二十週年結婚紀念。

Last Sunday, Mr. and Mrs. Wang went to a steakhouse to celebrate their 20th wedding anniversary.

✻ 結論句：這是難忘的一次經驗。

It is an unforgettable day for Mr. and Mrs. Wang and they will never forget it.

例二

One of Ben's hobbies is traveling. Of all the countries he has been to, he thinks Taiwan is the most attractive place. When he came to Taiwan for the first time many years ago, he was impressed with the beautiful scenery in Taiwan. He also liked the snacks at the night markets and appreciated the second tallest building, Taipei 101 in the world. When he comes to Taiwan again this June, he plans to go swimming and surfing at a beach.

✻ 主題句：Ben 的旅遊嗜好說明。

One of Ben's hobbies is traveling.

✻ 結論句：Ben 將再來一次臺灣玩。

When he comes to Taiwan again this June, he plans to go swimming and surfing at a beach.

例三

Taiwan has faced some economic difficulties in the past couple of years. As a result, a lot of people have seen their savings dwindle. Some people have lost their jobs. However, while the people here are worrying about whether or not they will be able to afford a long vacation overseas, most people in the world are worrying about whether or not they will have enough to sustain themselves. People in Taiwan need to appreciate what they have.

✻ 主題句：臺灣在過去幾年面臨經濟危機。

Taiwan has faced some economic difficulties in the past couple of years.

✻ 結論句：臺灣的人們要懂得感激現在所擁有的。

People in Taiwan need to appreciate what they have.

請找出主題句與結論句，並再閱讀一次本段落

練習題一

There are so many things that worry me. To be honest, I like a girl in my class, but she has a boyfriend who is tall, rich, charming and even has a convertible. In addition, my parents always lecture me, so I feel depressed and unhappy when I stay home. I don't know how to be happy, and I think I suffer from depression at times.

✻ 主題句是：

____

✻ 結論句是：

____

✻ 先猜測本文的內容，再閱讀整段，是否與所猜測的相同？

練習題二

There is only one earth, and we should do our best to protect it. First of all, recycle our old newspapers and magazines, so we don't waste paper and can save lots of trees. Secondly, carry our own bags while going shopping instead of using stores' plastic bags. In the third place, take the public transportation to work instead of driving your own car, and you can reduce air pollution. Above all, we rely on the only earth.

✻ 主題句是：

____

✻ 結論句是：

____

✻ 先猜測本文的內容，再閱讀整段，是否與所猜測的相同？

練習題三

English is an important and international language, so a good number of people are learning it. However, still many students think that it is difficult to practice English, especially for the speaking part. As a matter of fact, as long as they practice speaking English frequently and keep every chance that they can talk in English, they can overcome any difficulties. In conclusion, practice makes perfect. Never stop doing it!

✻ 主題句是：

____

✻ 結論句是：

____

✻ 先猜測本文的內容，再閱讀整段，是否與所猜測的相同？

解答 ANSWER

練習題一

There are so many things that worry me. To be honest, I like a girl in my class, but she has a boyfriend who is tall, rich, charming and even has a convertible. In addition, my parents always lecture me, so I feel depressed and unhappy when I stay home. I don't know how to be happy, and I think I suffer from depression at times.

✻ 主題句是：很多的事情困擾著我。

There are so many things that worry me.

✻ 結論句是：我不知如何快樂，有時我覺得自己得了憂鬱症。

I don't know how to be happy, and I think I suffer from depression at times.

練習題二

There is only one earth, and we should do our best to protect it. First of all, recycle our old newspapers and magazines, so we don't waste paper and can save lots of trees. Secondly, carry our own bags while going shopping instead of using stores' plastic bags. In the third place, take the public transportation to work instead of driving your own car, and you can reduce air pollution. Above all, we rely on the only earth.

✻ 主題句是：我們只有一個地球，我們應該竭盡所能地來保護它。

There is only one earth, and we should do our best to protect it.

✻ 結論句是：最重要的是，我們依賴這唯一的地球。

Above all, we rely on the only earth.

練習題三

English is an important and international language, so a good number of people are learning it. However, still many students think that it is difficult to practice English, especially for the speaking part. As a matter of fact, as long as they practice speaking English frequently and keep every chance that they can talk in English, they can overcome any difficulties. In conclusion, practice makes perfect. Never stop doing it!

✻ 主題句是：英文是重要且國際性的語言，所以很多人都正在學習它。
English is an important and international language, so a good number of people are learning it.

✻ 結論句是：總而言之，越練習英文會越好，所以永遠不要停止學習！
In conclusion, practice makes perfect. Never stop doing it!

2.3 閱讀力的提升：找出支持句Finding supporting sentences

在找出主題句與結論句之後，若是尚有時間來做進一步的閱讀，此時我們就要專注在支持句（supporting sentences）上。一般而言，支持句會出現在主題句與支持句之間，若是一個段落的閱讀，支持句就是主題句後的四到五句，而若是一篇五段式的長篇閱讀，支持的段落（supporting paragraphs）則會出現在二至四段。

例一

Last Sunday, Mr. and Mrs. Wang went to a steakhouse to celebrate their 20th wedding anniversary. While they were enjoying their meal, the fire alarm went off; then they saw the flames coming out of the kitchen. Mr. and Mrs. Wang rushed down the stairs to escape from this terrible fire. Soon, the fire engines arrived. A short time later, the fire was under control and everything was fine. It is an unforgettable day for Mr. and Mrs. Wang and they will never forget it.

✻ 支持句一：

While they were enjoying their meal, the fire alarm went off; then they saw the flames coming out of the kitchen.

✻ 支持句二：

Mr. and Mrs. Wang rushed down the stairs to escape from this terrible fire.

✻ 支持句三：

Soon, the fire engines arrived.

✻ 支持句四：

A short time later, the fire was under control and everything was fine.

例二

One of Ben's hobbies is traveling. Of all the countries he has been to, he thinks Taiwan is the most attractive place. When he came to Taiwan for the first time many years ago, he was impressed with the beautiful scenery in Taiwan. He also liked the snacks at the night markets and appreciated the second tallest building, Taipei 101 in the world. When he comes to Taiwan again this June, he plans to go swimming and surfing at a beach.

✻ 支持句一：

Of all the countries he has been to, he thinks Taiwan is the most attractive place.

✻ 支持句二：

When he came to Taiwan for the first time many years ago, he was impressed with the beautiful scenery in Taiwan.

✻ 支持句三：

He also liked the snacks at the night markets and appreciated the second tallest building, Taipei 101 in the world.

例三

Taiwan has faced some economic difficulties in the past couple of years. As a result, a lot of people have seen their savings dwindle. Some people have lost their jobs. However, while the people here are worrying about whether or not they will be able to afford a long vacation overseas, most people in the world are worrying about whether or not they will have enough to sustain themselves. People in Taiwan need to appreciate what they have.

✻ 支持句一：

As a result, a lot of people have seen their savings dwindle.

✻ 支持句二：

Some people have lost their jobs.

✻ 支持句三：

However, while the people here are worrying about whether or not they will be able to afford a long vacation overseas, most people in the world are worrying about whether or not they will have enough to sustain themselves.

請找出支持句，並再閱讀一次本段落

練習題一

There are so many things that worry me. To be honest, I like a girl in my class, but she has a boyfriend who is tall, rich, charming and even has a convertible. In addition, my parents always lecture me, so I feel depressed and unhappy when I stay home. I don't know how to be happy, and I think I suffer from depression at times.

✻ 支持句有：

____

____

____

____

練習題二

There is only one earth, and we should do our best to protect it. First of all, recycle our old newspapers and magazines, so we don't waste paper and can save lots of trees. Secondly, carry our own bags while going shopping instead of using stores' plastic bags. In the third place, take the public transportation to work instead of driving your own car, and you can reduce air pollution. Above all, we rely on the only earth.

✻ 支持句有：

____

____

____

____

練習題三

English is an important and international language, so a good number of people are learning it. However, still many students think that it is difficult to practice English, especially for the speaking part. As a matter of fact, as long as they practice speaking English frequently and keep every chance that they can talk in English, they can overcome any difficulties. In conclusion, practice makes perfect. Never stop doing it!

✻ 支持句有：

ANSWER

練習題一

There are so many things that worry me. To be honest, I like a girl in my class, but she has a boyfriend who is tall, rich, charming and even has a convertible. In addition, my parents always lecture me, so I feel depressed and unhappy when I stay home. I don't know how to be happy, and I think I suffer from depression at times.

✻ 支持句有：

1. To be honest, I like a girl in my class, but she has a boyfriend who is tall, rich, charming and even has a convertible.
2. In addition, my parents always lecture me, so I feel depressed and unhappy when I stay home.

練習題二

There is only one earth, and we should do our best to protect it. First of all, recycle our old newspapers and magazines, so we don't waste paper and can save lots of trees. Secondly, carry our own bags while going shopping instead of using stores' plastic bags. In the third place, take the public transportation to work instead of driving your own car, and you can reduce air pollution. Above all, we rely on the only earth.

✻ 支持句有：

1. First of all, recycle our old newspapers and magazines, so we don't waste paper and can save lots of trees.
2. Secondly, carry our own bags while going shopping instead of using stores' plastic bags.
3. In the third place, take the public transportation to work instead of driving your own car, and you can reduce air pollution.

練習題三

English is an important and international language, so a good number of people are learning it. However, still many students think that it is difficult to practice English, especially for the speaking part. As a matter of fact, as long as they practice speaking English frequently and keep every chance that they can talk in English, they can overcome any difficulties. In conclusion, practice makes perfect. Never stop doing it!

✽ 支持句有：

1. However, still many students think that it is difficult to practice English, especially for the speaking part.
2. As a matter of fact, as long as they practice speaking English frequently and keep every chance that they can talk in English, they can overcome any difficulties.

2.4 閱讀力的提升：組織時間順序 Time Order

大部分的故事短文或是敘述文，都是根據時間與事件發生的順序來做描述。換言之，若能找出文章中的「時間順序」（Time Order），對於閱讀的吸收會更加順暢。所以在閱讀這方面的文體時，時間與日期是讀者先要找到的關鍵字。再來，還有一些有關時間順序的「訊號字」（signal words），我們也要能掌握。常見文章中有關時間的訊號字有：

- **after** 後來
- **at last** 最後
- **before** 之前
- **finally** 最後
- **first** 第一
- **later** 之後
- **next** 接下來
- **second** 第二
- **then** 然後
- **when** 當時
- **while** 正當
- **as soon as** 一……就……

例一

I can hardly believe my good luck this month. ① At the beginning of the month, I got good grades for my mid-term examination. ② Then, grandparents gave me a brand new mobile phone and an innovative computer. ③ At the end of the month, I got the first place in an English writing contest. To be honest, I haven't been so happy before.

訊號字有：

① At the beginning of the month

② Then

③ At the end of the month

故事的發展順序為：

1. I got good grades for my mid-term examination.
2. My grandparents gave me a brand new mobile phone and an innovative computer.
3. I got the first place in an English writing contest.

例二

① When I was in high school, my body was very weak and I caught a cold so often. ② After beginning with university, I tried every opportunity to do more physical activities and training. ③ Two years later, physical training has made me not just taller but stronger. ④ Right now, people say that they cannot believe I used to be a weak man.

訊號字有：

① When I was in high school

② After beginning with university

③ Two years later

④ Right now

故事的發展順序為：

1. My body was very weak and I caught a cold so often.
2. I tried every opportunity to do more physical activities and training
3. Physical training has made me not just taller but stronger.
4. People say that they cannot believe I used to be a weak man.

請找出時間順序的訊號字，並將下列事件作先後次序的排列

I went for a night snack in the night market one day. First, I rode my bike to the night market. Then, I parked my bike and walked down the bustling street. Just a while later, I found trash that was piled everywhere. I thought that the garbage was filled with viruses after I saw it. In the end, I lost my appetite and went home directly.

✻ 時間順序的訊號字有：

____

____

✻ 將下列事件以數字 1～5 作先後次序的排列：

(　) I parked my bike and walked down the bustling street.

(　) I lost my appetite and went home directly.

(　) I thought that the garbage was filled with viruses.

(　) I rode my bike to the night market.

(　) I found trash that was piled everywhere.

解答 ANSWER

I went for a night snack in the night market one day. ① First, I rode my bike to the night market. ② Then, I parked my bike and walked down the bustling street. ③ Just a while later, I found trash that was piled everywhere. I thought that the garbage was filled with viruses ④ after I saw it. ⑤ In the end, I lost my appetite and went home directly.

✻ 時間順序的訊號字有：

First; Then; Just a while later; after I saw it; In the end

✻ 將下列事件以數字 1～5 作先後次序的排列：

(2) I parked my bike and walked down the bustling street.

(5) I lost my appetite and went home directly.

(4) I thought that the garbage was filled with viruses.

(1) I rode my bike to the night market.

(3) I found trash that was piled everywhere.

2.5 閱讀力的提升：了解事實與意見 Distinguish facts and opinions

在閱讀時，另一個閱讀技巧我們應特別注意的是找出文章中的句子，究竟是「事實」(Facts)，或者這是作者個人的意見或是想法(Opinions)。這樣有助於讓你知道作者寫一篇文章的立場，也可以了解到作者運用什麼樣的知識、報告或是數字來佐證並支持他的論點。以下我們分別就事實與意見的句子說明。

事實（Facts）的例句：

1. Taipei 101 is the second tallest building in the world.
2. Architect Frank Gehry designed the Walt Disney Concert Hall.
3. According to the report, the hurricane last week caused over 3000 people homeless.
4. Over the 70% of the surface on earth is water.
5. My class consists of 50 students.

意見（Opinions）的例句：

1. Many people like watching comedy movie on the weekend.
2. I think the concert we went to last night is the best one ever.
3. Tom Cruise is so handsome.
4. The people of Los Angeles are happy about the Walt Disney Concert Hall.
5. Studying at the café is much more efficient than studying in my room.

例一

I grew up in a small village. At that time, there was a clear stream near my home. However, the stream is so dirty now that no fish can live anymore. <u>According to some information, we have to wait at least 10 years to have a clean</u>

stream. Frankly speaking, I don't know when I can see the beautiful scenes in my childhood again. I think people should do more, such as donations, to help us to have a new stream again.

✻ 事實（Facts）的例句：According to some information, we have to wait at least 10m years to have a clean stream.

✻ 意見（Opinions）的例句：I think people should do more, such as donations, to help us to have a new stream again.

例二

A color test can tell you about your personality. For instance, if you like blue, you tend to be calm. On the contrary, if you like red, you may like to take risks. In fact, a report that was released seven days ago said that 87% of the people who like red love taking risks or do some extreme sports. However, I have a friend who likes red, but really timid. Therefore, I think a color test may be different for different people. What's your idea?

✻ 事實（Facts）的例句：In fact, a report that was released seven days ago said that 87% of the people who like red love taking risks or do some extreme sports.

✻ 意見（Opinions）的例句：Therefore, I think a color test may be different for different people.

練習題 EXERCISES

請判斷以下段落中的句子是「事實」或是「意見」

According to recent studies, 38% of men in Taiwan smoke. These numbers are low when compared with China. In China, around 74% of all males have this habit. There are several reasons as to why fewer men in Taiwan smoke. For one reason, the government here has run many advertisements encouraging young people to stop smoking. I think people may be affected when seeing these ads. Certain laws also make it difficult for smoking in public. If you smoke in public, you will be fined $3200. Indeed, there is a lot of pressure on people who smoking. Also, if we can make these people quit smoking, we will have a cleaner environment than before.

請圈出「事實」或「意見」

1. 事實？意見？According to recent studies, 38% of men in Taiwan smoke.
2. 事實？意見？In China, around 74% of all males have this habit.
3. 事實？意見？I think people may be affected when seeing these ads.
4. 事實？意見？If you smoke in public, you will be fined $3200.
5. 事實？意見？If we can make these people quit smoking, we will have a cleaner environment than before.

解答 ANSWER

According to recent studies, 38% of men in Taiwan smoke. These numbers are low when compared with China. In China, around 74% of all males have this habit. There are several reasons as to why fewer men in Taiwan smoke. For one reason, the government here has run many advertisements encouraging young people to stop smoking. I think people may be affected when seeing these ads. Certain laws also make it difficult for smoking in public. If you smoke in public, you will be fined $3200. Indeed, there is a lot of pressure on people who smoking. Also, if we can make these people quit smoking, we will have a cleaner environment than before.

1. 事實 / According to recent studies, 38% of men in Taiwan smoke.
2. 事實 / In China, around 74% of all males have this habit.
3. 意見 / I think people may be affected when seeing these ads.
4. 事實 / If you smoke in public, you will be fined $3200.
5. 意見 / If we can make these people quit smoking, we will have a cleaner environment than before.

2.6 閱讀力的提升：因果關係的確認 Cause and Effect

還有一項閱讀技巧，我們稱之為因果關係的確認（Cause and Effect）。由於一般的文章閱讀都會說明事情的因果關係與來龍去脈，閱讀測驗中也常問"Why"，因此，找出事情的「因」，成為閱讀上的一大重點。

以下的例句中我們將句子列出，並找出它的「因」：

(1) **As a result of police's requirements, the man has been taken into the police station.** 因為警方的要求，這人被帶到警局去了。

因：police's requirements

果：the man has been taken into the police station

(2) **Because I was tired, I didn't go.** 因為我很累，所以我沒有去。

因：I was tired

果：I didn't go

(3) **Mary got that job because she was the best interviewee.** 瑪莉得到工作是因為她是最棒的面試者。

因：she was the best interviewee

果：Mary got that job

(4) **Charles was absent from work because of sickness.** 查爾斯缺席是因為他生病。

因：sickness

果：Charles was absent from work

(5) **Cancer may result from smoking frequently.** 癌症可能因經常吸煙造成。

因：smoking frequently

果：Cancer

(6) **Maria's hardworking attitude leads to a big success.** 瑪利亞因為認真工作的態度而導致大成功。

因：Maria's hardworking attitude

果：a big success

(7) **The failure was due to careless attitude.** 這失敗是由於不小心的態度。

因：careless attitude

果：The failure

(8) **Our manager retired on account of poor health.** 我們的經理因健康不佳而退休。

因：poor health

果：Our manager retired

(9) **As a result of the complaint, the shop owner decided to finish the business.** 由於抱怨，商店所有者決定結束營業。

因：the complaint

果：the shop owner decided to finish the business.

(10) **The delay was due to the bad weather.** 這延遲是由於不良的氣候造成。

因：the bad weather

果：The delay

例一

There are many reasons why I love movies. The main reason is that it's the best way to relax myself. According to the reports, many people go to the movies at least once a month, and I am no exception. Another reason is that it's also the best way to date with my girlfriend. She likes movies, too. Finally, I think many movies can reflect real life experiences, so, that is to say, I learn something from the movie I see.

因：it's the best way to relax myself. + it's also the best way to date with my girlfriend.+ I think many movies can reflect real life experiences.

果：I love movies

練習題 EXERCISES

請判斷以下段落中的句子是「因」或是「果」

Many students pay so little attention to their study methods that they waste their time. They have been studying English for many years, but they still cannot understand rather easy articles. The reason is that they always choose too difficult or too boring articles to read. Additionally, they often consult the dictionary as soon as they run into new words rather than "guess" them first. This bad reading habit causes that the readers cannot read something quickly. Also, in some kinds of reading tests, they cannot finish reading articles in time.

請圈出「因」或「果」

1. 因？果？Many students pay so little attention to their study methods.
2. 因？果？They waste their time.
3. 因？果？They always choose too difficult or too boring articles to read.
4. 因？果？They still cannot understand rather easy articles.
5. 因？果？They often consult the dictionary as soon as they run into new words rather than "guess" them first.
6. 因？果？The readers cannot read something quickly.
7. 因？果？They cannot finish reading articles in time.

解答 ANSWER

Many students pay so little attention to their study methods that they waste their time. They have been studying English for many years, but they still cannot understand rather easy articles. The reason is that they always choose too difficult or too boring articles to read. Additionally, they often consult the dictionary as soon as they run into new words rather than "guess" them first. This bad reading habit causes that the readers cannot read something quickly. Also, in some kinds of reading tests, they cannot finish reading articles in time.

1. 因 / Many students pay so little attention to their study methods.
2. 果 / They waste their time.
3. 因 / They always choose too difficult or too boring articles to read.
4. 果 / They still cannot understand rather easy articles.
5. 因 / They often consult the dictionary as soon as they run into new words rather than "guess" them first.
6. 果 / The readers cannot read something quickly.
7. 果 / They cannot finish reading articles in time.

2.7 閱讀力的提升：掃描與略讀 Scanning and Skimming

在這一節中，我們將練習閱讀文章時，為了要節省時間看出文章的重點，所需運用的閱讀技巧：

第一類（掃描－看字）

文章中，經常出現的重複字詞，通常就是我們要注意的關鍵重要字詞。以下我們先做一組練習，請找出每一題中的重複字。

1. near / nearly / next / nest / never / nearer / nest

   答 ?

2. five / live / fine / fit / fix / fist / fine

   答 ?

3. think / thank / thin / ring / thank / tank / rein

   答 ?

4. light / right / might / right / fight / tight / night

   答 ?

5. owe / own / owl / out / owes / owl / our

   答 ?

6. pie / lie / die / tie / put / pit / pie

   答 ?

7. law / paw / lax / lawn / lawn / last / caw

   答 ?

8. except / exception / accept / inception / excel / accept

   答 ?

9. cut out / cut off / cut in / cut down / calm down / put off / cut in

   答 ?

10. fist name / first name / last name / full name / surname / first name

    答 ?

解答 ANSWER

1. near / nearly / next / nest / never / nearer / nest

   答 nest

2. five / live / fine / fit / fix / fist / fine

   答 fine

3. think / thank / thin / ring / thank / tank / rein

   答 thank

4. light / right / might / right / fight / tight / night

   答 right

5. owe / own / owl / out / owes / owl / our

   答 owl

6. pie / lie / die / tie / put / pit / pie

   答 pie

7. law / paw / lax / lawn / lawn / last / caw

   答 lawn

8. except / exception / accept / inception / excel / accept

   答 accept

9. cut out / cut off / cut in / cut down / calm down / put off / cut in

   答 cut in

10. fist name / first name / last name / full name / surname / first name

    答 first name

第二類（略讀－看句）

請先閱讀以下的題目，然後到段落中尋找答案。

1. What do people believe in?
2. What does the word "ghost" mean?
3. Why are people afraid of them?

> Without doubt, there are many strange things that people believe in. As far as I know, in many countries people believe in ghosts. Ghosts are spirits of people who have died. Some people say that they have seen or heard them, and most people are afraid of them because they look frightening.

答案：

1. There are many strange things.
2. Spirits of people who have died.
3. Because they look frightening.

2.8 閱讀力的提升：掌握轉折詞 Transitions 與代名詞 Pronouns

從閱讀的角度來學英文，還有兩個非常重要的詞類，就是轉折詞（Transition）與代名詞（Pronoun）。這兩個詞性將左右閱讀者對於文章的理解力與透析度。以下我們分別作介紹。

-Noticing transitions（轉折詞）

英文文章中根據上下句之間的邏輯關係，會有最恰當的轉折詞。轉折詞如一潤滑劑般，其目的在於告知下一句的性質與立場。一般而言，轉折詞分為以下數類，分述如下：

項目	常考轉折詞
1. 還有類（表繼續）	**and, also, in addition, second, again, moreover, furthermore, first**
2. 然而類（改變語氣）	**but, however, nevertheless, yet, still, notwithstanding, on the other hand**
3. 例如類（舉例）	**for example, for instance, in other words, in particular**
4. 類似類（與後面類同）	**in a like manner, likewise, in the same way, in a similar case, similarly**
5. 肯定類（語氣肯定）	**indeed, in fact, as a matter of fact, truly, I repeat, certainly, admittedly, no doubt**
6. 總結類（作結論）	**to sum up, in conclusion, in short, finally, in summary, in sum, to make a long story short**
7. 讓步類（雖然）	**Though, although, it may be true that, even though, granted that**
8. 因此類（表結果）	**therefore, consequently, hence, then, thus, as a consequence**

我們來看這一段有關「找工作回覆」的例子：

We just received your resume and found you had excellent background and the work experience and bachelor's degree in business you have are just what we want. However, the opening you're interested is already filled. Therefore, we cannot offer you any positions in our company now.

本段中出現兩個轉折詞，"however" 表達的即是「改變語氣」。段落前部分強調應徵者的優勢，但是"however"的出現，讓我們知道「工作無望了」！"therefore"，則是表示「結果」，結果即是「目前公司無法提供任何的職缺」。

例一 （劃底線處為轉折詞）

I usually go to the country on the weekend. In addition, I like watching people. But last weekend I had a change. I decided to visit the park near my home. I left home early, therefore, the whole city was so quiet. However, when I arrived at the park, I was surprised to see so many people there. Believe it or not, some people were feeding the fish in the pond, and others were sitting on the park bench. What's more, a lot of people were jogging. Everybody was so energetic there. In short, that was really a special experience for me.

例二 （劃底線處為轉折詞）

Last autumn, my family and I took a vacation in Germany. However, none of us could speak German. As a consequence, at the restaurants or the train stations, we used hand gestures to order food and get some tickets. To my surprise, all the German we met were all polite and friendly, and it sure was an unforgettable experience. To sum up, I think that we will definitely visit there again soon.

練習題 EXERCISES

請填入 first / in addition / then / however / finally

Lisa was very busy today. ________, she went to school and took eight classes. ________, she also did some part-time work at school. In class, she wrote some important notes on paper. ________, she went to the library to find some books she needed. ________, she couldn't find them. ________, she gave up and went straight home. What a day it was.

ANSWER

Lisa was very busy today. First, she went to school and took eight classes. In addition, she also did some part-time work at school. In class, she wrote some important notes on paper. Then, she went to the library to find some books she needed. However, she couldn't find them. Finally, she gave up and went straight home. What a day it was.

-Noticing pronouns（代名詞）

要能了解英文文章中的代名詞，才能迅速正確的閱讀一篇文章。以下我們用一段文字來說明了解代名詞的重要性。

例一 （代名詞的練習）

Pronouns are small but important words. (1)They can replace nouns. Writers often use pronouns, so (2)they don't have to repeat the same nouns over and over. Good readers look for pronouns when (3)they read. (4)They also look for the nouns that (5)they refer to. This helps (6)them read faster and understand more.

其中 (1) 至 (6) 所代表的名詞，分別是：

(1) pronouns

(2) writers

(3) readers

(4) readers

(5) pronouns

(6) readers

請寫出以下代名詞所代替的名詞

例一

Everyone in my family is a doctor. My father works at General Hospital, and (1)he is a physician. (2)He needs to keep in touch with the hospital. (3)He always carries his cell phone. My mother used to work in the hospital, but (4)she doesn't anymore. Now, (5)she is an assistant professor. (6)She teaches medicine at a university. I want to be a doctor, too. I will study medicine. I will study at the university where my mother works. I want (7)her to teach me.

(1) ________ (2) ________

(3) ________ (4) ________

(5) ________ (6) ________

(7) ________

例二

Scientists have been telling us that the environment is in danger. Although (1)they give us warnings, most people continue to waste energy and resources. (2)They use air-conditioners twenty-four hours a day and drive everywhere all the time. It's hard to say when (3)they take environmental issues seriously. According to some recent reports, the environment is polluted seriously, and (4)they also tell us that one day we will no long live on earth. (5)It will "die" soon. In short, we have to care (6)it before something terrible happens and stop polluting (7)it any more.

(1) ________ (2) ________

(3) ________ (4) ________

(5) ________ (6) ________

(7) ________

例一

Everyone in my family is a doctor. My father works at General Hospital, and (1)he is a physician. (2)He needs to keep in touch with the hospital. (3)He always carries his cell phone. My mother used to work in the hospital, but (4)she doesn't anymore. Now, (5)she is an assistant professor. (6)She teaches medicine at a university. I want to be a doctor, too. I will study medicine. I will study at the university where my mother works. I want (7)her to teach me.

(1) my father (2) my father

(3) my father (4) my mother

(5) my mother (6) my mother

(7) my mother

例二

Scientists have been telling us that the environment is in danger. Although (1)they give us warnings, most people continue to waste energy and resources. (2)They use air-conditioners twenty-four hours a day and drive everywhere all the time. It's hard to say when (3)they take environmental issues seriously. According to some recent reports, the environment is polluted seriously, and (4)they also tell us that one day we will no long live on earth. (5)It will "die" soon. In short, we have to care (6)it before something terrible happens and stop polluting (7)it any more.

(1) scientists (2) most people

(3) most people (4) reports

(5) earth (6) earth

(7) earth

2.9 閱讀力的提升：其他常見閱讀測驗應注意的事項

以下再列舉 17 點閱讀到不同的文體應注意的部分：

1. 郵件：主旨和姓氏。
2. 販售：期間。
3. 行程：行程中變與不變的內容。
4. 徵人廣告：徵的職位、條件、福利、如何應徵。
5. 問卷：評論、問的項目。
6. 長條圖：所涵蓋的時間。
7. 文章：主題句與結論句。
8. 圓餅圖：百分比的比較。
9. 留言：誰來電？要找誰？誰接的。
10. 雙篇閱讀要找出衝突點與相同處。
11. 前後句子間的邏輯關係常會利用連接詞或轉折詞來呈現，例如：and、or、but、so、if、after、before、since、when、because、besides、however、although、otherwise、therefore 等，熟悉連接詞的運用，有助於理解整篇文章的脈絡。
12. 瀏覽並找出主題句。
13. 看結論句了解作者立場。
14. 先看題目，注意疑問詞。
15. 注意關鍵字，特別是代名詞。
16. 轉折詞了解語氣的轉換。
17. 答案採刪去法。

TWO

PART 2

閱讀測驗實戰練習

Chapter 3

段落填空題型題目介紹

這一個章節我們將了解目前各大英文考試的閱讀測驗題型。第一個部分是段落填空，在這類的考題中，考生要練習閱讀的速度，並在閱讀的過程中，了解字詞的涵義，也將句型與文法的概念同時納入，更重要的是單句與單句間的語氣轉折，因此轉折詞也是這類考試題型常出現的重點。第二個部分則是閱讀文章，這個部分涵蓋很廣，不僅是一般文章分為敘述文、議論文、說明文與描寫文等文體之外，常見的應用英文文體，如書信（又分生活書信與商業書信），以及英文的公告、告示、備忘錄、索引、菜單、警告標語等題材琳瑯滿目都會出現在這類的考題中，近年又因多益閱讀考試出現雙篇閱讀的題型，這類新的題型演練也是十分重要的。

第一組題目

One of my reasons for coming to Taiwan is to experience living in a different culture and to ___(1)___ new ways of thinking about life. Although I would say that I have a good relationship with my parents, I have not lived with either of them ___(2)___ I was 18. In North America, actually, people might think that there is something wrong ___(3)___ a single woman of 30 who still lives at home. I think that any of them are lacking in independence or in the ability to ___(4)___ themselves. We would say that the ___(5)___ of someone's independence is his or her ability to live away from family and survive. For this reason, I think I make a right decision to come to Taiwan and live here alone.

---

(1) Ⓐ be exposed to　Ⓑ be composed of
　Ⓒ be supposed to　Ⓓ be opposed to

(2) Ⓐ because　Ⓑ although
　Ⓒ since　Ⓓ from

(3) Ⓐ to care for　Ⓑ to call off
　Ⓒ to stand by　Ⓓ to put into

(4) Ⓐ of　Ⓑ with
　Ⓒ in addition to　Ⓓ by

(5) Ⓐ measurement　Ⓑ measuring
　Ⓒ measure　Ⓓ measures

第一組中文翻譯與解答解析

我來到臺灣的原因之一是想要體驗生活在不一樣的風俗因而使對生活新的思考方式能夠被挖掘出來。雖然我跟我父母有不錯的關係，但自從我十八歲的時候我就沒有跟他們任何一位住在一起了。事實上在北美洲，人們可能會想說這樣一個三十幾歲的單身女子還住在父母的家中一定是有什麼問題。我覺得她們缺少獨立自主的個性或者是缺少照顧她們自己的能力。我們會說測量一個人的自主性就是他或她擁有離開家裡獨自生活及生存的能力。因為這個原因，我認為我做了正確的決定，來到臺灣並獨居。

---

(1) Ⓐ be exposed to（暴露於） Ⓑ be composed of（由……組成）
Ⓒ be supposed to（應該） Ⓓ be opposed to（反對）
解 Ⓐ（本句是說要體驗新的生活，將自己暴露於或說接觸新的事物並體驗新的人生。）

(2) Ⓐ because（因為） Ⓑ although（雖然）
Ⓒ since（自從） Ⓓ from（從）
解 Ⓒ（自從十八歲之後就再也沒與父母同居。）

(3) Ⓐ to care for（照顧） Ⓑ to call off（取消）
Ⓒ to stand by（支持） Ⓓ to put into（投入）
解 Ⓐ（本句是「照顧」他們自己的意思。）

(4) Ⓐ of Ⓑ with
Ⓒ in addition to Ⓓ by
解 Ⓑ（wrong 後加 with 介詞。）

(5) Ⓐ measurement（尺寸、大小 n.）
Ⓑ measuring（measure 的動名詞）
Ⓒ measure（測量 v. / n.）
Ⓓ measures（measure 為不可數名詞）
解 Ⓒ（由 the measure of 判斷是測量的意思，名詞用法。）

第二組題目

Most people in the United States live in big cities, and there is a certain ___(1)___ for them about spending spare time in the countryside. The ultimate fantasy includes buying an older cabin and being able to renovate it to your own tastes. ___(2)___ a desire maybe comes from an idea that one is re-living the pioneer experience of the original European settlers in North America. The goal of all this renovation is to create a place where every corner is a ___(3)___ retreat. How does it work? The trick is to keep the rustic feel of a cabin in the woods ___(4)___ being able to enjoy all the conveniences of modern living. The trouble is that few people have the time, money or skills to make their weekend cabin dream a reality. It's not uncommon to find a family cabin that has been "under ___(5)___" for years. The reason is because the owners only have a few weekends each summer to spend working on their property.

---

(1) Ⓐ romantic Ⓑ romancing
Ⓒ romance Ⓓ romances

(2) Ⓐ Such Ⓑ So
Ⓒ That Ⓓ It's

(3) Ⓐ lazy Ⓑ crazy
Ⓒ cozy Ⓓ busy

(4) Ⓐ while Ⓑ because
Ⓒ if Ⓓ although

(5) Ⓐ construction Ⓑ restriction
Ⓒ district Ⓓ contraction

第二組中文翻譯與解答解析

大部分在美國的人都住在大城市，所以他們對於在鄉村度過他們的休閒時光有種絕對的羅曼蒂克想法。這終極的幻想包含買一個比較舊的休閒小屋而且能夠用自己的喜好來重新裝潢它。這樣的渴望大概是來自於想要重新體驗歐洲早期殖民者在北美洲開拓經驗的想法。這些重新裝潢小屋的目標是要去創造一個地方。在那裡，每一個角落都是溫馨的私人空間。而這要如何執行？設計的祕訣就是將小屋的鄉村風情保存在樹林中同時也能夠享受所有現代化生活所帶來的便利。但問題在於只有少部分的人有錢、時間或技藝去創造一個真正屬於他們夢想的週末小屋。所以發現一間「建造中」的房子是很平常的事，原因是這些小屋的擁有者每年夏天只有幾個週末來進行房子的工程。

(1) Ⓐ romantic（浪漫的 adj.） Ⓑ romancing
Ⓒ romance（浪漫 n.） Ⓓ romances（浪漫 n.）
解 Ⓒ（本句是 a certain 開頭，後應該加名詞的單數。）

(2) Ⓐ Such Ⓑ So
Ⓒ That Ⓓ It's
解 Ⓐ（本句是說「這樣的」…所以要用"such a" 來作表達）

(3) Ⓐ lazy（懶惰的） Ⓑ crazy（瘋狂的）
Ⓒ cozy（舒適的） Ⓓ busy（忙碌的）
解 Ⓒ（根據文意，本句是指溫馨舒適的個人空間。）

(4) Ⓐ while（當；同時） Ⓑ because（因為）
Ⓒ if（假如） Ⓓ although（雖然）
解 Ⓒ（本句是說一邊可以……同一時間又可以……。）

(5) Ⓐ construction（建造 n.） Ⓑ restriction（限制 n.）
Ⓒ district（地區 n.） Ⓓ contraction（收縮 n.）
解 Ⓐ（under construction 是「建造中」的意思。）

第三組題目

Many people study English for years, and they can talk to the occasional foreigners or get around with ease when they travel ___(1)___ English speaking countries. However, many people still tend to struggle is in their attempt to write clearly in English. One great way to improve writing skill is just to read a lot in English. This will help you become more ___(2)___ common grammar structures and increase your vocabulary. The other thing that it is essential to do is to write! "Practice makes perfect," ___(3)___ they say. ___(4)___ a regular writing time for yourself by taking a class, picking up a writing workbook or just trying to exchange English e-mail with friends. Then give your work to someone and ask for his or her opinions. Don't be afraid of ___(5)___. Having other people point out your weak areas is necessary if you want to correct problems. Yes, let us write now!

(1) Ⓐ in Ⓑ on
Ⓒ beyond Ⓓ beneath

(2) Ⓐ similar to Ⓑ familiar with
Ⓒ equipped with Ⓓ superior to

(3) Ⓐ as Ⓑ as if
Ⓒ when Ⓓ that

(4) Ⓐ Create Ⓑ Creating
Ⓒ To create Ⓓ Created

(5) Ⓐ critics Ⓑ critiques
Ⓒ criticism Ⓓ critters

第三組中文翻譯與解答解析

很多人學習英文很多年，而他們可以跟偶爾碰面的外國人溝通，或者當他們到英語系的國家旅行時，他們可以很輕鬆的到處去逛。然而，很多人仍傾向於在寫清楚的作文中，辛苦的掙扎。一個很棒的方法來改善你的寫作技巧就是閱讀英文。這將幫助你對一些普通的文法結構更加熟悉而且還會增加你的單字量。另一件必要的事情就是要去寫，正如一般人所說的「熟能生巧」。利用加入課程、使用寫作練習簿或是試著寄英文電子郵件給朋友們來建立一個屬於你自己的寫作時間。然後將你的文章給某人過目以徵求他或她的意見。不要害怕被批評。如果你想要更正問題的話，有其他人來指出你的弱點是必要的。是的，讓我們開始寫作吧。

(1) Ⓐ in（在裡面） Ⓑ on（在上面）
Ⓒ beyond（之外） Ⓓ beneath（之下）
解 Ⓐ（在國家要用 “in” a country。）

(2) Ⓐ similar to（相似） Ⓑ familiar with（熟悉）
Ⓒ equipped with（裝配） Ⓓ superior to（優於）
解 Ⓑ（本句的意思是閱讀可以幫助你對一些普通的文法結構更加的熟悉，所以要用 familiar with 片語。）

(3) Ⓐ as（如同 conj.） Ⓑ as if（猶如、好像）
Ⓒ when（當conj.） Ⓓ that（因為 conj.）
解 Ⓐ（as 是如同的意思。）

(4) Ⓐ Create Ⓑ Creating
Ⓒ To create Ⓓ Created
解 Ⓐ（create 使用動詞原型開頭的句型，為命令句的用法。）

(5) Ⓐ critics（評論家 n.） Ⓑ critiques（評論文章 n.）
Ⓒ criticism（批評、批判 n.） Ⓓ critters（異常的動物 n.）
解 Ⓒ（criticism 是批判的意思。）

第四組題目

I have a dog, and I love it so much. Dogs have a long-time relationship with human beings. I think that dogs are diligent, loyal and cute animals. They are human beings' companions and servants as well. When we are ___(1)___ them, they are faithful to us and standing by us. When their masters are attacked, they bark at the masters' foe loudly, and even attack him. Dogs are ___(2)___ snobbish; They never ___(3)___ their masters because they're poor or sick. Some dogs even ___(4)___ tombs of their deceased masters until they die for starvation. In addition, dogs are also useful animals. Basically, all dogs can watch our home, and they can also help in hunting. They can detect drugs, and even ___(5)___ whether there are lives under the ruins. As you can see, dogs are really our loyal friends.

(1) Ⓐ lack of　　Ⓑ in need of
　　Ⓒ need　　Ⓓ needed

(2) Ⓐ in all ways　　Ⓑ by all means
　　Ⓒ in no way　　Ⓓ not at all

(3) Ⓐ dessert　　Ⓑ desert
　　Ⓒ decent　　Ⓓ detergent

(4) Ⓐ guard　　Ⓑ guide
　　Ⓒ garage　　Ⓓ gardening

(5) Ⓐ sniff　　Ⓑ snore
　　Ⓒ smoke　　Ⓓ smell

第四組中文翻譯與解答解析

我有一隻狗，我非常喜歡牠。狗和人類有著深遠的關係，我覺得狗是勤勉的、忠心的、可愛的動物，牠們是人類的夥伴也是僕人。當我們需要他們時，他們總會在我們身邊。如果主人遭到襲擊，牠們會對敵人大聲吠叫，甚至還會攻擊敵人。小狗絕不是很勢利的動物，他們從不會在主人貧困或生病時離棄主人，有些狗甚至會守護亡主的墳墓，直到自己餓死為止。此外，狗也是有用的動物。基本而言，所有的狗都會看家，而且會幫忙狩獵，他們會緝毒甚至在事故現場嗅出生還者的氣息。就你所看到的，狗真的是人類最忠實的朋友。

(1) Ⓐ lack of（缺乏）
Ⓑ in need of（需要）
Ⓒ need（需要 v.）
Ⓓ needed（need 的過去式／過去分詞）
解 Ⓑ（in need of +名詞，為有需要的意思。）

(2) Ⓐ in all ways（通過各種方法） Ⓑ by all means（一定）
Ⓒ in no way（絕不） Ⓓ not at all（一點也不）
解 Ⓒ（in no way = by no means 表示絕不的意思。）

(3) Ⓐ dessert（點心 n.） Ⓑ desert（沙漠 n. / 遺棄 v.）
Ⓒ decent（正派的 adj.） Ⓓ detergent（使潔淨的 adj.）
解 Ⓑ（desert 遺棄*動詞用法。）

(4) Ⓐ guard（守衛 v.） Ⓑ guide（引導 v.）
Ⓒ garage（車庫 n.） Ⓓ gardening（園藝 n.）
解 Ⓐ（guard 守衛*動詞用法。）

(5) Ⓐ sniff（嗅 v.） Ⓑ snore（打鼾 v.）
Ⓒ smoke（抽煙 v.） Ⓓ smell（聞 v.）
解 Ⓐ（sniff 嗅*動詞用法。）

第五組題目

Do you want a job? Do you want to have a successful interview? Here are some tips you have to know more. The ___(1)___ you make when walking into the room is absolutely important. When you prepare for your interview, try to ___(2)___ whether the company has some dressing codes. Then you must dress ___(3)___ their regulations. Then, the interviewer will have a good commend on you. As a good interviewee, you also need to prepare lots of questions to ask the interviewer. That will make interviewer think you are well prepared. Some common questions are ___(4)___ the future development in the company. Of course, a good interviewee will ask questions about ___(5)___, like salary and benefits. That's crucial, isn't it?

(1) Ⓐ impressionism Ⓑ imprison
Ⓒ impressive Ⓓ impression

(2) Ⓐ find out Ⓑ research
Ⓒ look up to Ⓓ now that

(3) Ⓐ according to Ⓑ in addition to
Ⓒ in need of Ⓓ accord

(4) Ⓐ disregard Ⓑ regarding
Ⓒ regardless of Ⓓ regarding about

(5) Ⓐ compensation Ⓑ companion
Ⓒ conference Ⓓ conglomerate

第五組中文翻譯與解答解析

你想要一份工作嗎？想要有一個成功的面試嗎？這裡有一些你需要知道多一點的祕訣。在你走進房間時給人的印象是非常重要的。在面談之前，你應該試著找出公司對穿著打扮的習慣，然後依據這些原則打扮自己，我相信這麼做的話，面試官會給你很高的評價。身為一位好的面談者，你也必須準備很多的問題來問面試官。這會讓面試官認為你有十足的準備。一些常見的問題是有關於在公司未來的發展。當然，一位好的應徵者會問有關薪酬的問題，就像是月薪與福利等。那是非常重要的，不是嗎？

---

(1) Ⓐ impressionism（印象主義 n.） Ⓑ imprison（監禁 v.）
Ⓒ impressive（印象深的 adj.） Ⓓ impression（印象 n.）
解 Ⓓ（impression 印象*名詞用法。）

(2) Ⓐ find out（找出） Ⓑ research（研究 v.）
Ⓒ look up to（尊敬） Ⓓ now that（既然）
解 Ⓐ（find out 找出。）

(3) Ⓐ according to（根據） Ⓑ in addition to（除此之外）
Ⓒ in need of（需要） Ⓓ accord（協議 n.）
解 Ⓐ（in accordance with = according to 根據。）

(4) Ⓐ disregard（忽視 v.）
Ⓑ regarding（有關於 prep.）
Ⓒ regardless of（不管、不顧 prep.）
Ⓓ regarding about
解 Ⓑ（regarding 有關於。）

(5) Ⓐ compensation（薪酬 n.） Ⓑ companion（陪伴 n.）
Ⓒ conference（會議 n.） Ⓓ conglomerate（企業集團 n.）
解 Ⓐ（compensation 薪資與福利的總合，薪酬的意思。）

第六組題目

Mary,

Mrs. Lee called while you were out. She said that she had to drop her daughter ___(1)___ at the clinic tonight, so she couldn't walk with you to the yoga class as planned. ___(2)___, she said she would meet you there. She also wanted me to remind you to bring the pan that you promised to ___(3)___ to her. Also, Mr. Wong called you, too. He said he had your car ___(4)___, and you can pick your car anytime tomorrow. He wanted you to call him back ___(5)___ your convenience.

Lillian

---

(1) Ⓐ in　　Ⓑ off
　Ⓒ down　　Ⓓ over

(2) Ⓐ Instead　　Ⓑ Insist
　Ⓒ Instant　　Ⓓ Instance

(3) Ⓐ borrow　　Ⓑ borrowing
　Ⓒ lend　　Ⓓ lending

(4) Ⓐ repair　　Ⓑ repaired
　Ⓒ to repair　　Ⓓ was repairing

(5) Ⓐ in　　Ⓑ on
　Ⓒ at　　Ⓓ above

第六組中文翻譯與解答解析

瑪莉：

妳出去的時候李太太來電，她說她今晚必須要送她女兒去診所，所以她不能依約和妳一起走路去上瑜伽課，而是和妳直接在課堂上碰面。她還要我提醒妳，要記得帶妳答應要借給她的鍋子。而且，王先生也有來電。他說已經把妳的車修好了，妳可以明天任何時刻去取車。他要妳方便的時候回他電話。

莉莉安

---

(1) Ⓐ in　　Ⓑ off

Ⓒ down　　Ⓓ over

解 Ⓑ（drop off...，代表送某人……的意思。）

(2) Ⓐ Instead（相反地 adv.）　　Ⓑ Insist（堅持 v.）

Ⓒ Instant（立即的 adj.）　　Ⓓ Instance（例子 n.）

解 Ⓐ（instead 表相反的，轉折詞的用法。）

(3) Ⓐ borrow（借入 v.）　　Ⓑ borrowing

Ⓒ lend（借出 v.）　　Ⓓ lending

解 Ⓒ（promise + to 動詞原形，為保證或答應之意。lend 借出，borrow 則是借入的意思。）

(4) Ⓐ repair（修理 v.）　　Ⓑ repaired

Ⓒ to repair　　Ⓓ was repairing

解 Ⓑ（have 使役動詞的用法，使役動詞後接物，再加上的動詞要用過去分詞表示被動。）

(5) Ⓐ in　　Ⓑ on

Ⓒ at　　Ⓓ above

解 Ⓒ（at your convenience 是「以你方便為主」的意思。）

第七組題目

You probably don't know that your roosters ___(1)___ too early, and it really disturbs us. We're considering calling 911, so please solve this problem as soon as possible. ___(2)___, your dog is always biting my cat and running in my courtyard. Please clean up the ___(3)___ it did. We can't stand it anymore.

___(4)___ thanks for your help.

___(5)___ yours,

Your neighbors.

---

(1) Ⓐ bark Ⓑ crow
Ⓒ crawl Ⓓ shout

(2) Ⓐ Beside Ⓑ Besides
Ⓒ Further Ⓓ Furthermore

(3) Ⓐ mass Ⓑ mess
Ⓒ messy Ⓓ missing

(4) Ⓐ Marry Ⓑ Many
Ⓒ Much Ⓓ May

(5) Ⓐ Sincere Ⓑ Sincerely
Ⓒ Faithful Ⓓ Best regards

第七組中文翻譯與解答解析

你也許不知道你的公雞叫得太早了，而且真的打擾了我們。我們正考慮要打 911 報警，請你盡快改善這種情形。此外，你的狗總是愛咬我的貓，並在我的院子裡奔跑，請清乾淨牠所弄得一團亂。我們再也受不了了。

十分感謝你的幫忙。

真誠地祝福你

你的鄰居敬上

---

(1) Ⓐ bark（狗吠 v.） Ⓑ crow（公雞啼 v.）
Ⓒ crawl（爬 v.） Ⓓ shout（大叫 v.）

解 Ⓑ（crow 公雞啼*動詞用法。）

(2) Ⓐ Beside（在旁邊 prep.）
Ⓑ Besides（此外 adv.）
Ⓒ Further（更進一步地 adv.）
Ⓓ Furthermore（更進一步地 adv.）

解 Ⓑ（besides 此外*副詞，在這裡有語氣轉折的用途。）

(3) Ⓐ mass（大眾 n.） Ⓑ mess（一團亂 n.）
Ⓒ messy（一團亂adj.） Ⓓ missing（不見了 adj.）

解 Ⓑ（這裡指狗弄得一團亂。）

(4) Ⓐ Marry（嫁娶 v.） Ⓑ Many（很多 adj.）
Ⓒ Much（很多 adj.） Ⓓ May（可能 aux.）

解 Ⓑ（many thanks 表示十分感謝。）

(5) Ⓐ Sincere（真誠的 adj.） Ⓑ Sincerely（真誠地 adv.）
Ⓒ Faithful（忠誠的 adj.） Ⓓ Best regards（問好）

解 Ⓑ（sincerely yours 結尾語，真誠地的意思。）

第八組題目

Julia,

I need to run out and pick up a few things, but I'll be home again before dinner. Do your homework and help ___(1)___ to a small snack. Also, I put some clothes in the ___(2)___ to make them dry. Please check on it when you're finished your homework and ___(3)___ them. Moreover, please go to the balcony ___(4)___ the plants and flowers. Don't forget to do these ___(5)___ before I come back.

Mom

(1) Ⓐ you Ⓑ yours
Ⓒ yourself Ⓓ yourselves

(2) Ⓐ dryer Ⓑ refrigerator
Ⓒ oven Ⓓ dishwasher

(3) Ⓐ find Ⓑ fold
Ⓒ foal Ⓓ folding

(4) Ⓐ to water Ⓑ watering
Ⓒ water Ⓓ watered

(5) Ⓐ chores Ⓑ choices
Ⓒ chalk Ⓓ chew

第八組中文翻譯與解答解析

茱莉亞，

我必須趕緊出門去拿一些東西，但是我將會在晚餐以前回來。做你的功課還有自己拿零食來吃。我放了一些衣服在烘乾機裡面讓它們乾。當你寫完功課的時候請幫我確認一下並把它們摺好。此外，請到陽台上澆花與植物。別忘了在我回來之前完成這些家事。

媽媽

---

(1) Ⓐ you Ⓑ yours

Ⓒ yourself Ⓓ yourselves

解 Ⓒ（help yourself 請自助，要用反身代名詞。）

(2) Ⓐ dryer（烘乾機 n.） Ⓑ refrigerator（電冰箱 n.）

Ⓒ oven（烤箱 n.） Ⓓ dishwasher（洗碗機 n.）

解 Ⓐ（dryer 是烘乾機的意思，表示要把衣服放在烘乾機裡烘乾。）

(3) Ⓐ find（發現 v.） Ⓑ fold（摺衣服 v.）

Ⓒ foal Ⓓ folding（摺衣服 Ving形式）

解 Ⓑ（fold 為摺衣服的意思，用動詞原形）

(4) Ⓐ to water Ⓑ watering

Ⓒ water Ⓓ watered

解 Ⓐ（go to the balcony to water 是指到陽台去做澆花的動作，要用不定詞來做表達。）

(5) Ⓐ chores（家事 n.） Ⓑ choices（選擇 n.）

Ⓒ chalk（粉筆 n.） Ⓓ chew（嚼 v.）

解 Ⓐ（do these chores 是指做一些家事。）

第九組題目

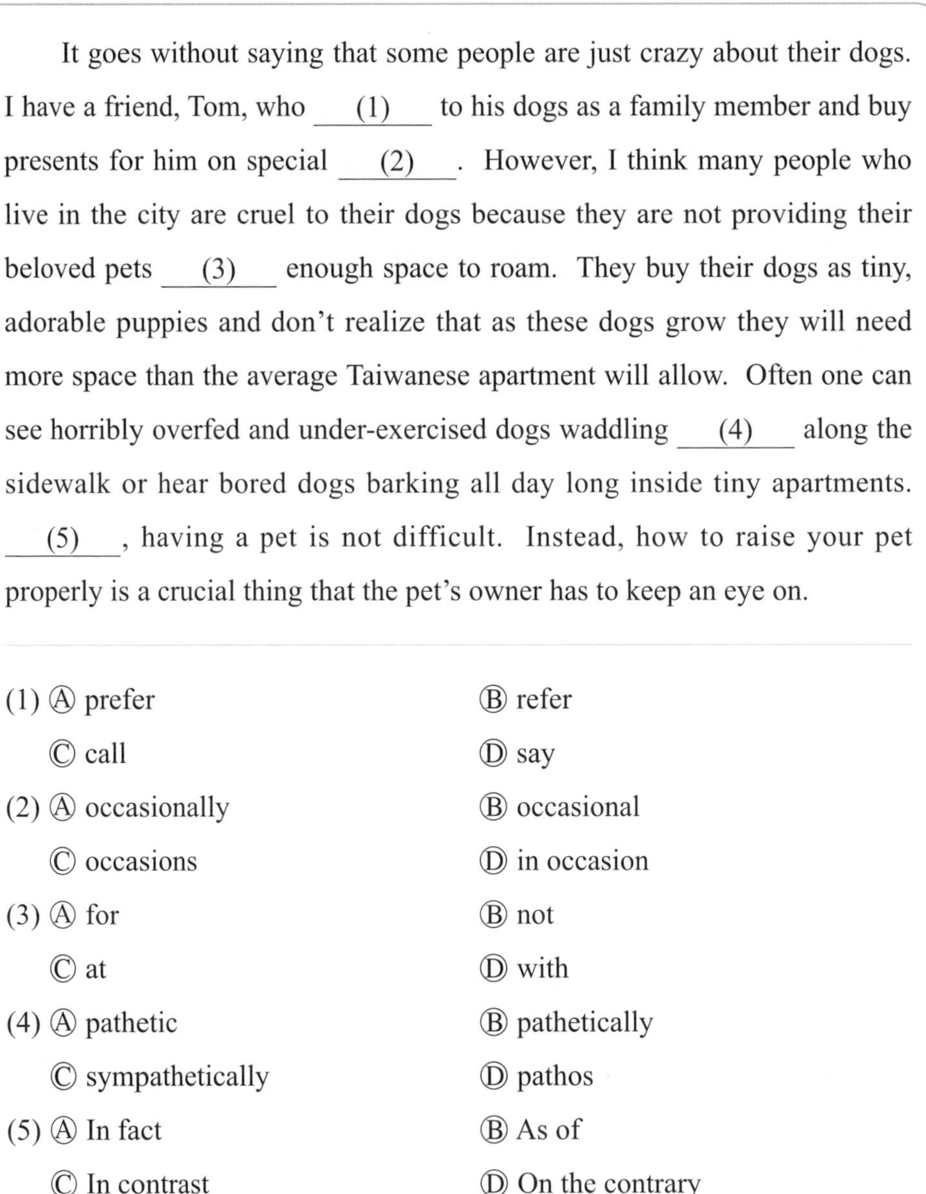

It goes without saying that some people are just crazy about their dogs. I have a friend, Tom, who ___(1)___ to his dogs as a family member and buy presents for him on special ___(2)___. However, I think many people who live in the city are cruel to their dogs because they are not providing their beloved pets ___(3)___ enough space to roam. They buy their dogs as tiny, adorable puppies and don't realize that as these dogs grow they will need more space than the average Taiwanese apartment will allow. Often one can see horribly overfed and under-exercised dogs waddling ___(4)___ along the sidewalk or hear bored dogs barking all day long inside tiny apartments. ___(5)___, having a pet is not difficult. Instead, how to raise your pet properly is a crucial thing that the pet's owner has to keep an eye on.

(1) Ⓐ prefer　Ⓑ refer
　Ⓒ call　Ⓓ say

(2) Ⓐ occasionally　Ⓑ occasional
　Ⓒ occasions　Ⓓ in occasion

(3) Ⓐ for　Ⓑ not
　Ⓒ at　Ⓓ with

(4) Ⓐ pathetic　Ⓑ pathetically
　Ⓒ sympathetically　Ⓓ pathos

(5) Ⓐ In fact　Ⓑ As of
　Ⓒ In contrast　Ⓓ On the contrary

第九組中文翻譯與解答解析

不用說，有些人對他們的小狗瘋狂著迷。我有一個朋友，湯姆，將他的小狗視為家中成員的一份子，而且在特別時刻會買禮物給小狗。然而，我覺得許多住在城市中的人對小狗很殘酷，因為他們沒有足夠空間可供他們喜愛的小狗走動。他們買下小狗時，牠們還是嬌小可愛的幼犬，而且沒有認知到當小狗長大以後，牠們需要更大的活動空間，這已經超過一般臺灣公寓的容許範圍。常常可以看到嚴重餵食過量且運動不足的小狗，可憐兮兮地沿著人行道蹣跚而行，或是聽到無聊的小狗在狹小的公寓裡整天叫個不停。事實上，擁有寵物並不難，相反的，如何適當地養你的寵物才是寵物主人要注意的重要事項。

---

(1) Ⓐ prefer（寧願 v.） Ⓑ refer（視為 v.）
Ⓒ call（叫 v.） Ⓓ say（說 v.）
解 Ⓑ（refer to 視為。）

(2) Ⓐ occasionally（偶爾 adv.） Ⓑ occasional（偶爾 adj.）
Ⓒ occasions（時刻 n.） Ⓓ in occasion（偶爾 adv.）
解 Ⓒ（occasions 時刻。）

(3) Ⓐ for Ⓑ not
Ⓒ at Ⓓ with
解 Ⓓ（provide...with... 提供……東西。）

(4) Ⓐ pathetic（可憐的 adj.）
Ⓑ pathetically（可憐地 adv.）
Ⓒ sympathetically（富有同情心地 adv.）
Ⓓ pathos（痛苦 n.）
解 Ⓑ（pathetically 可憐地。）

(5) Ⓐ In fact（事實上） Ⓑ As of（到了…時候）
Ⓒ In contrast（相反地） Ⓓ On the contrary（相反地）
解 Ⓐ（In fact 事實上。）

第十組題目

Do you like living in a foreign country? Traveling to foreign countries ___(1)___ a willingness to try things that are different and uncommon. I believe this based on my current experiences as a foreigner working in Taipei and the kinds of foreigners I meet from Western countries here. I would describe one kind as successful and the others as unsuccessful simply based on the differences in their willingness to try new things.

Some people wish to ___(2)___ their lives from home here in Taipei, make a lot of money and then leave. ___(3)___ my best friend as an example, he wants to make a lot of money by teaching English in Taiwan, so he has many teaching hours a week, nevertheless, he actually spends more money ___(4)___ western luxuries to comfort his frustrated and unhappy feeling all day. Therefore, if you really want to have a good life in a foreign country, try to understand some different cultures and ___(5)___ some unnecessary culture shocks!

---

(1) Ⓐ requires　Ⓑ required
　Ⓒ requirement　Ⓓ requiring

(2) Ⓐ duplicate　Ⓑ extravagance
　Ⓒ contagious　Ⓓ intoxicate

(3) Ⓐ Take　Ⓑ Make
　Ⓒ Have　Ⓓ Regain

(4) Ⓐ in　Ⓑ by
　Ⓒ with　Ⓓ on

(5) Ⓐ keep track of　Ⓑ keep up with
　Ⓒ keep away from　Ⓓ keep an eye on

第十組中文翻譯與解答解析

你喜歡住在國外嗎？出國旅行需要有嘗試新奇與不同事物的意願，我會相信這一點是根據最近我身為在臺北工作者的外國人，以及我在這裡遇見來自西方國家的各國人。我可以說其中一群是成功的，另一群是失敗的，就是根據他們嘗試新事物的意願，以及最後因異國生活經驗而做出改變的意願。有些人希望把他們的生活方式複製到臺灣來，只想賺了大筆鈔票之後就離開。就拿我最好的朋友當作例子，他想藉由在臺灣教英文而賺很多錢，所以他一週有很多的教學時數，然而，他卻花費大筆的錢在西式的奢侈上來安慰他一整天的沮喪和不開心的感覺。因此，假如你真的想要在外國過愉快的生活，要去試著了解不同的文化以及避免一些不必要的文化衝擊。

(1) Ⓐ requires Ⓑ required
Ⓒ requirement Ⓓ requiring
解 Ⓐ（require 要求*動詞用法。）

(2) Ⓐ duplicate（複製 v.） Ⓑ extravagance（奢侈品 n.）
Ⓒ contagious（有傳染力的 adj.） Ⓓ intoxicate（中毒 v.）
解 Ⓐ（duplicate 複製*動詞用法。）

(3) Ⓐ Take Ⓑ Make
Ⓒ Have Ⓓ Regain
解 Ⓐ（take... as an example，以……當作例子。）

(4) Ⓐ in Ⓑ by
Ⓒ with Ⓓ on
解 Ⓓ（spend on+ 物，在……上的花費。）

(5) Ⓐ keep track of（保持紀錄） Ⓑ keep up with（跟上）
Ⓒ keep away from（避免） Ⓓ keep an eye on（注意）
解 Ⓒ（本句是說要避免文化衝擊。）

第十一組題目

English is an international language, for it is ___(1)___ used in the world. English is important not only because it is a language of commerce, science and technology, ___(2)___ because it is an international language of communication. Now ___(3)___ many new words are becoming a part of the English vocabulary that English may be called "an ___(4)___ language." Practically, supposing you want a good job, you must ___(5)___ English. Many companies offer some good jobs that ask for some TOEIC or GEPT certificates. That is, it'll be harder and harder to find a good job in Taiwan if you don't have some competitive edges.

(1) Ⓐ wide Ⓑ widely Ⓒ width Ⓓ wild

(2) Ⓐ but only Ⓑ only also Ⓒ also Ⓓ but also

(3) Ⓐ such Ⓑ so Ⓒ so that Ⓓ such as

(4) Ⓐ exploring Ⓑ experience Ⓒ export Ⓓ expert

(5) Ⓐ good at Ⓑ adept at Ⓒ have a good command of Ⓓ make a good use of

第十一組中文翻譯與解答解析

英文是國際語言，因為它在世界各地被廣泛地使用。英文的重要不只是因為它在商業、科學和科技上的使用，還因為它是國際用以溝通的語言。現今已有這麼多的新字成為英文字彙的一部分，英文可以被稱為是「爆炸的語言」了。實際上，假如你想要找一份好的工作，你必須擁有良好的英文運用能力，很多公司提供好的工作機會，但大多要求多益或是全民英檢的證照。也就是說，假如你沒有一些競爭優勢的話，要在臺灣找一份好的工作是越來越難了。

---

(1) Ⓐ wide（廣泛的 adj.）　Ⓑ widely（廣泛地 adv.）
Ⓒ width（寬度 n.）　Ⓓ wild（野生的 adj.）
解 Ⓑ（widely 廣泛地*副詞用法。）

(2) Ⓐ but only　Ⓑ only also
Ⓒ also　Ⓓ but also
解 Ⓓ（not only... but also... 不但……而且。）

(3) Ⓐ such　Ⓑ so
Ⓒ so that　Ⓓ such as
解 Ⓑ（so...that... 太……以至於……。）

(4) Ⓐ exploring（爆炸的 adj.）　Ⓑ experience（經驗 n.）
Ⓒ export（輸出 v.）　Ⓓ expert（專家 n.）
解 Ⓐ（exploring 爆炸的*形容詞用法。）

(5) Ⓐ good at（擅長 adj.）
Ⓑ adept at（擅長 adj.）
Ⓒ have a good command of（有良好的運用能力 v.）
Ⓓ make a good use of（利用、善用 v.）
解 Ⓒ（have a good command of 表示有良好的運用能力。）

第十二組題目

Check that your writing makes sense:

1. Does your essay have a topic sentence?
2. Do you write enough supporting sentences to support your topic sentence?
3. Is it correctly ___(1)___ on the page?
4. Is your information presented clearly, ___(2)___ a logical order?
5. Make sure you have put in all the information your reader needs.
6. Have you put in any unnecessary information?
7. Can you replace any words with more ___(3)___ vocabulary?
8. Check spelling and ___(4)___.
9. Correct any grammatical mistakes and ___(5)___ your sentence patterns.

Next time, when you try to write a composition, do not forget these nine points.

---

(1) Ⓐ organization Ⓑ organized
Ⓒ organize Ⓓ organizing

(2) Ⓐ in Ⓑ for
Ⓒ from Ⓓ off

(3) Ⓐ precise Ⓑ predict
Ⓒ present Ⓓ prepared

(4) Ⓐ punctuation Ⓑ punctual
Ⓒ punch Ⓓ bunch

(5) Ⓐ vary Ⓑ various
Ⓒ very Ⓓ variety

第十二組中文翻譯與解答解析

確定你的文章是有意義的：

1. 你的文章有主題句嗎？
2. 你有足夠的支持句來支持你的主題句嗎？
3. 文章是正確地被組織在頁面中嗎？
4. 你是不是清楚地、合乎邏輯地陳述你的資料。
5. 確定你已經把所有讀者所需的資訊寫進文章中。
6. 你是不是寫了不必要的資訊？
7. 你是不是可以用更精確的字彙取代文章中的任何字眼？
8. 檢查拼字和標點符號有無錯誤。
9. 修正文法錯誤並多變化你的句型。

下一次當你需要寫一篇作文時，不要忘記這九個重點。

---

(1) Ⓐ organization　Ⓑ organized
Ⓒ organize　Ⓓ organizing

解 Ⓑ（organized 被組織，被動語態 be+Vpp。）

(2) Ⓐ in　Ⓑ for
Ⓒ from　Ⓓ off

解 Ⓐ（in a logical way 以一個合乎邏輯的方式。）

(3) Ⓐ precise（精準的 adj.）　Ⓑ predict（預測 v.）
Ⓒ present（目前的 adj)　Ⓓ prepared（有準備的 adj.）

解 Ⓐ（precise 精準的*形容詞用法。）

(4) Ⓐ punctuation（標點符號 n.）　Ⓑ punctual（正確的 adj.）
Ⓒ punch（用拳猛擊 v.）　Ⓓ bunch（一束 n.）

解 Ⓐ（punctuation 標點符號*名詞用法。）

(5) Ⓐ vary（變化 v.）　Ⓑ various（多變的 adj.）
Ⓒ very（非常 adv.）　Ⓓ variety（多樣性 n.）

解 Ⓐ（vary 變化的意思*動詞用法。）

第十三組題目

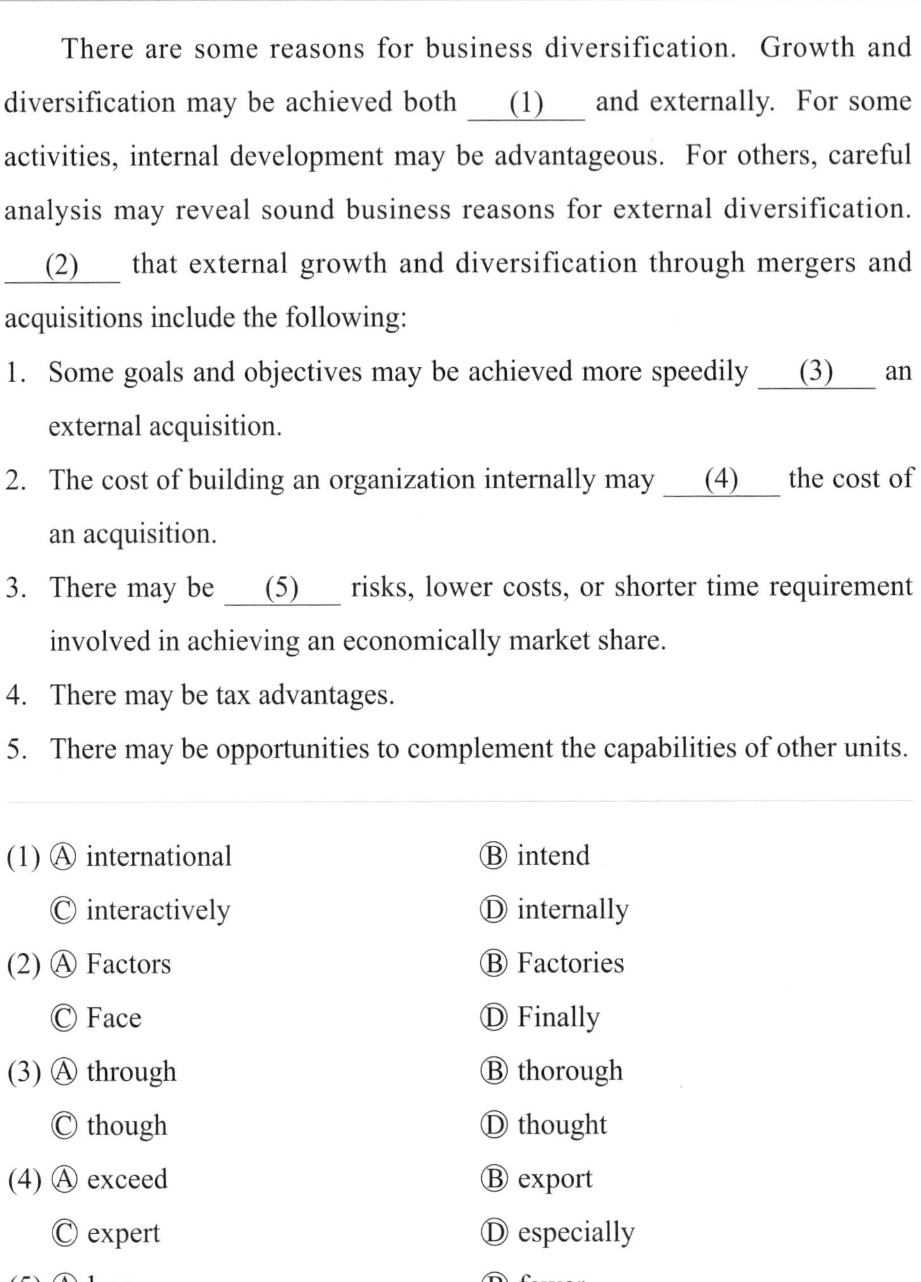

There are some reasons for business diversification. Growth and diversification may be achieved both ___(1)___ and externally. For some activities, internal development may be advantageous. For others, careful analysis may reveal sound business reasons for external diversification. ___(2)___ that external growth and diversification through mergers and acquisitions include the following:

1. Some goals and objectives may be achieved more speedily ___(3)___ an external acquisition.
2. The cost of building an organization internally may ___(4)___ the cost of an acquisition.
3. There may be ___(5)___ risks, lower costs, or shorter time requirement involved in achieving an economically market share.
4. There may be tax advantages.
5. There may be opportunities to complement the capabilities of other units.

---

(1) Ⓐ international　　Ⓑ intend
　　Ⓒ interactively　　Ⓓ internally

(2) Ⓐ Factors　　Ⓑ Factories
　　Ⓒ Face　　Ⓓ Finally

(3) Ⓐ through　　Ⓑ thorough
　　Ⓒ though　　Ⓓ thought

(4) Ⓐ exceed　　Ⓑ export
　　Ⓒ expert　　Ⓓ especially

(5) Ⓐ less　　Ⓑ fewer
　　Ⓒ more　　Ⓓ the most

第十三組中文翻譯與解答解析

有一些原因會促進商業經營的多角化。公司內部和外部的運作都可以達到公司的成長及多樣化的經營。有些活動可能對內部成長有利。對其他活動而言，謹慎的分析可能會發現一個健全企業對多角化經營的動機。藉由合併和收購來達成外部成長和多樣化經營的因素包括下列所示：

1. 有些目標和願景可以透過外部收購更快速的達成。
2. 內部建造和組織的費用可能超過了收購的費用。
3. 達成經濟市場的分享可能風險比較低、費用比較少，或是需要的時間較短。
4. 可能有賦稅優惠。
5. 有機會補足其他單位的人才。

---

(1) Ⓐ international（國際的 adj.）　Ⓑ intend（打算 v.）
Ⓒ interactively（互相作用地 adv.）Ⓓ internally（內部地 adv.）
解 Ⓓ（internally 內部地*副詞用法。）

(2) Ⓐ Factors（因素 n.）　Ⓑ Factories（工廠 n.）
Ⓒ Face（面對 v.）　Ⓓ Finally（最後 adv.）
解 Ⓐ（Factors 因素*名詞用法。）

(3) Ⓐ through（透過 prep.）　Ⓑ thorough（仔細的 adj.）
Ⓒ though（雖然 conj.）　Ⓓ thought（想 v.）
解 Ⓐ（through 透過。）

(4) Ⓐ exceed（超過 v.）　Ⓑ export（出口 v.）
Ⓒ expert（專家 n.）　Ⓓ especially（特別地 adv.）
解 Ⓐ（exceed 超過*動詞用法。）

(5) Ⓐ less（較少的 adj.）　Ⓑ fewer（較少的 adj.）
Ⓒ more（較多的 adj.）　Ⓓ the most（最多的）
解 Ⓑ（fewer + 可數名詞。）

第十四組題目

Students are afraid of tests. ___(1)___ a test or an examination is approaching, they start to get nervous. On the eve of tests, they usually worry that they will fail to their tests, so they burn the midnight oil in the hope that they ___(2)___ get better grades. As a matter of fact, tests just are part of students'lives. Why should they be afraid? As students, they ought to study hard and prepare their own for future careers. So I think that a test is only used to test whether a student is ___(3)___. According to a ___(4)___ of high school students across the nation, 90% of them stay up late before the day of the exam. In my opinion, when you know that a test is coming, you ought to relax yourself. When you relax yourself, you can develop your any kinds of abilities and potential, you will find that it is so easy for you to answer all questions on your test sheets, because relaxation is a kind of lubricant that can make your memory machine run smoothly. So nervousness during the examination period can only ___(5)___ negative effect.

(1) Ⓐ Whatever Ⓑ Whenever
Ⓒ Whichever Ⓓ However

(2) Ⓐ can be able to Ⓑ be able to
Ⓒ will can Ⓓ will be able to

(3) Ⓐ fully-prepared Ⓑ totally-wanted
Ⓒ absolutely-gained Ⓓ extremely- scared

(4) Ⓐ conference Ⓑ survey
Ⓒ science Ⓓ forecast

(5) Ⓐ production Ⓑ productive
Ⓒ productivity Ⓓ produce

第十四組中文翻譯與解答解析

學生都懼怕測驗。每當接近測驗或考試的日子，他們就會開始緊張。在考試的前一天晚上，他們經常會擔心自己會考得不好，所以熬夜念書希望能獲得更好的成績。事實上，測驗只是學生生活的一部分。為什麼學生要害怕考試呢？作為一個學生，應該是要努力讀書，為自己將來就業好好準備。所以我認為測驗只是用來評量學生是否預備妥當罷了。根據一個跨國性高中學生的調查顯示，百分之九十的人都在考試前一天熬夜。就我的觀點來看，在接近考試的時候你應該要放輕鬆。放輕鬆的時候，你將能夠發揮你的任何一種能力和潛力，你會發現對你而言，回答考試卷上的題目是這麼的容易，因為放輕鬆是一種潤滑劑，它會讓你的記憶機械順利運作。所以，在考試期間緊張只會產生負面效果。

(1) Ⓐ Whatever（無論什麼） Ⓑ Whenever（無論何時）
Ⓒ Whichever（無論是哪一個） Ⓓ However（無論如何）
解 Ⓑ（whenever無論何時。）

(2) Ⓐ can be able to Ⓑ be able to
Ⓒ will can Ⓓ will be able to
解 Ⓓ（will be able to 將能夠。）

(3) Ⓐ fully-prepared（完整準備的 adj。）
Ⓑ totally-wanted（完全想要的 adj。）
Ⓒ absolutely-gained（絕對有收穫的 adj。）
Ⓓ extremely- scared（極端恐懼的 adj。）
解 Ⓐ（fully-prepared 完整準備的。）

(4) Ⓐ conference（會議 n.） Ⓑ survey（調查 n.）
Ⓒ science（科學 n.） Ⓓ forecast（預測 n.）
解 Ⓑ (survey 調查。）

(5) Ⓐ production（產品 n.） Ⓑ productive（多產的 adj.）
Ⓒ productivity（生產力 n.） Ⓓ produce（生產 v.）
解 Ⓓ（produce 生產。）

第十五組題目

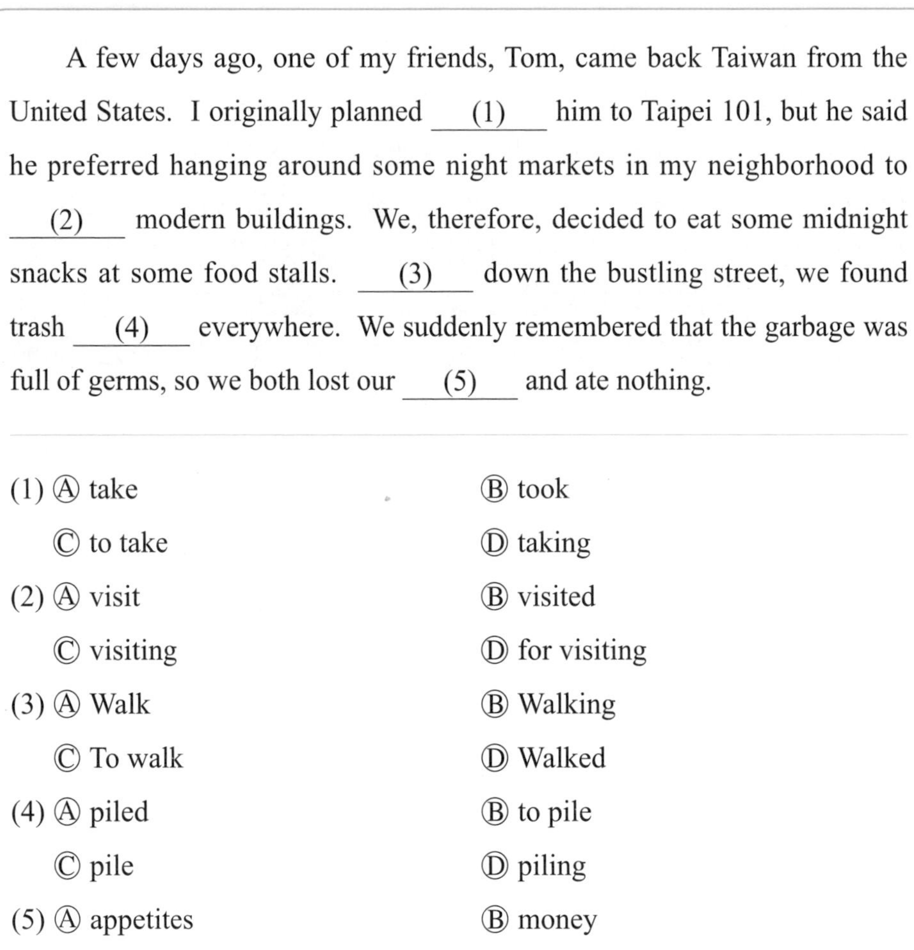

A few days ago, one of my friends, Tom, came back Taiwan from the United States. I originally planned ___(1)___ him to Taipei 101, but he said he preferred hanging around some night markets in my neighborhood to ___(2)___ modern buildings. We, therefore, decided to eat some midnight snacks at some food stalls. ___(3)___ down the bustling street, we found trash ___(4)___ everywhere. We suddenly remembered that the garbage was full of germs, so we both lost our ___(5)___ and ate nothing.

(1) Ⓐ take Ⓑ took Ⓒ to take Ⓓ taking

(2) Ⓐ visit Ⓑ visited Ⓒ visiting Ⓓ for visiting

(3) Ⓐ Walk Ⓑ Walking Ⓒ To walk Ⓓ Walked

(4) Ⓐ piled Ⓑ to pile Ⓒ pile Ⓓ piling

(5) Ⓐ appetites Ⓑ money Ⓒ stools Ⓓ energy

第十五組中文翻譯與解答解析

前幾天，我的一位朋友，Tom，從美國回到臺灣。我原本計畫帶他到臺北101，但是他說他喜歡到我家附近的一些夜市逛逛甚於參觀現代的建築物。因此，我們決定在小吃攤吃一些宵夜。當我們走在熱鬧的街上時，我們發現到處堆滿了垃圾。我們突然想起這些垃圾都充滿了病菌，所以我們都失去胃口，什麼都沒吃。

---

(1) Ⓐ take　　Ⓑ took
　Ⓒ to take　　Ⓓ taking
　解 Ⓒ（plan + to V 原形。）

(2) Ⓐ visit　　Ⓑ visited
　Ⓒ visiting　　Ⓓ for visiting
　解 Ⓒ（prefer Ving to Ving。）

(3) Ⓐ Walk　　Ⓑ Walking
　Ⓒ To walk　　Ⓓ Walked
　解 Ⓑ（Walking down the... 是 When we walked down the... 的分詞構句。）

(4) Ⓐ piled　　Ⓑ to pile
　Ⓒ pile　　Ⓓ piling
　解 Ⓐ（piled 指垃圾被堆放，有被動的意思。）

(5) Ⓐ appetites（胃口 n.）　　Ⓑ money（錢 n.）
　Ⓒ stools（板凳 n.）　　Ⓓ energy（精力 n.）
　解 Ⓐ（本句中是指失去胃口，不想吃東西。）

第十六組題目

The most important purpose of advertising is to ___(1)___ the customers of some products or services. The second purpose is to sell products. And the second purpose is utterly important to manufactures. Due to advertisement, consumers think they really need this thing and buy it then. After ___(2)___, sometimes the consumers complained themselves, "Why do I need them?" The ___(3)___ commercial I have ever watched on TV is the one that has a cute baby lying in a rocking bed. When the bed rocks forward, we see the baby laugh. When the bed rocks back, we see the baby cry. However, we hear no words. At the last part of the commercial, we finally see what the baby sees. The baby ___(4)___ a store's sign when the bed rocks forward. Then, the baby cries ___(5)___ he can't catch the sign when the bed rocks back.

(1) Ⓐ information Ⓑ acknowledge
Ⓒ be informed Ⓓ be acknowledged

(2) Ⓐ bought Ⓑ buy
Ⓒ buying Ⓓ buing

(3) Ⓐ impressed Ⓑ the most impressive
Ⓒ impressive Ⓓ the most impressed

(4) Ⓐ catches Ⓑ deserts
Ⓒ revolves Ⓓ conserves

(5) Ⓐ because Ⓑ although
Ⓒ due to Ⓓ despite

第十六組中文翻譯與解答解析

廣告最重要的目的在於告知消費者有某些產品在銷售，次要的目的在於銷售產品，而且這次要的目的對製造商來說是十分重要的，消費者因為看了廣告而覺得自己真的需要這樣產品，然後就會去購買。有時候消費者在購買之後會埋怨自己：「為什麼我會需要這些東西呢？」我曾經看過印象最深刻的廣告是有一個可愛小孩躺在搖籃上。當搖籃向前時，我們看見小孩笑，當搖籃向後時，我們看見小孩哭。然而，我們什麼都聽不到。到了廣告的最後，我們看見小孩看見的東西。當床向前搖時，小孩看見了商店的招牌，然後小孩哭了，因為在床向後搖時，他看不到招牌。

---

(1) Ⓐ information（資訊 n.）　Ⓑ acknowledge（告知 v.）

Ⓒ be informed（被通知）　Ⓓ be acknowledged（被告知）

解 Ⓑ（acknowledge 告知*動詞用法。）

(2) Ⓐ bought　Ⓑ buy

Ⓒ buying　Ⓓ buing

解 Ⓒ（after+Ving 分詞構句。）

(3) Ⓐ impressed　Ⓑ the most impressive

Ⓒ impressive　Ⓓ the most impressed

解 Ⓑ（the most impressive 最深刻的。）

(4) Ⓐ catches（抓到、看到 v.）　Ⓑ deserts（拋棄 v.）

Ⓒ revolves（旋轉 v.）　Ⓓ conserves（保存 v.）

解 Ⓐ（catches 抓到；看到*動詞用法。）

(5) Ⓐ because（因為 conj.）　Ⓑ although（雖然 conj.）

Ⓒ due to（由於 prep.）　Ⓓ despite（雖然 prep.）

解 Ⓐ（because + 子句。）

第十七組題目

To whom it may concern,

This a letter to inform you that my mailing address has ___(1)___. Please update your files accordingly and arrange to have all my monthly ___(2)___ and other notices sent to the new address. My new address, effective immediately, is: 3rd Floor, #177 Park Road, Da-an District, Taipei City 102. Thank you for taking care of this request. I can be contacted ___(3)___ 5555-8341 ___(4)___ you have any questions.

PS: Please by regular mail, not by ___(5)___ due to the fact that I'm frequently away from home. Many thanks for your help.

---

(1) Ⓐ change Ⓑ changing
Ⓒ changes Ⓓ changed

(2) Ⓐ statements Ⓑ conglomerate
Ⓒ massages Ⓓ work

(3) Ⓐ of Ⓑ with
Ⓒ at Ⓓ for

(4) Ⓐ should Ⓑ could
Ⓒ would Ⓓ shall

(5) Ⓐ registering Ⓑ certified
Ⓒ certify Ⓓ register

第十七組中文翻譯與解答解析

給相關注意人士：

這是一封提醒您我的郵件地址已經改變的信件。請據此更新你的檔案然後整理所有我的月結清單跟其他注意事項郵寄到我的新地址。我的新地址：102 臺北市大安區公園路 177 號 3 樓，立即生效。謝謝您對這項要求的注意。有任何問題的話您可以打 5555-8341 的電話聯絡我。

備註：請以一般郵件，不要用掛號郵件寄出，因為我經常不在家中。多謝您的幫忙。

---

(1) Ⓐ change　Ⓑ changing
Ⓒ changes　Ⓓ changed

解 Ⓓ（has changed 已經改變；have / has+ Vp.p.現在完成式。）

(2) Ⓐ statements（對帳單 n.）　Ⓑ conglomerate（企業集團 n.）
Ⓒ massages（按摩 n.）　Ⓓ work（工作 n.）

解 Ⓐ（statements 對帳單。）

(3) Ⓐ of　Ⓑ with
Ⓒ at　Ⓓ for

解 Ⓒ（at + 電話號碼。）

(4) Ⓐ should　Ⓑ could
Ⓒ would　Ⓓ shall

解 Ⓐ（Should you have any questions 是 If you should have any questions 的倒裝句。）

(5) Ⓐ registering　Ⓑ certified
Ⓒ certify　Ⓓ register

解 Ⓑ（certified mail 與 registered mail 為掛號信的兩種說法。）

第十八組題目

To: All employees

From: Sharon Lee, Office Manager

I'm sending this as a reminder of our departmental meeting scheduled for 9a.m. next Thursday. Here is a ___(1)___ agenda.

10:00a.m.	___(2)___ of new staff members
10:15a.m.	Review the previous meeting minutes
10:30a.m.	Quarterly reports
10:50a.m.	Strategic planning: Merger with 3H Company
11:30a.m.	Organize the planning ___(3)___
12:00p.m.	Adjourn

Please ___(4)___ me by 5:00p.m. on Tuesday if you have ___(5)___ agenda items as I will be distributing the confirmed agenda on Wednesday afternoon.

(1) Ⓐ draft Ⓑ drafting
Ⓒ drafts Ⓓ daft

(2) Ⓐ introduce Ⓑ introduction
Ⓒ interact Ⓓ interaction

(3) Ⓐ committee Ⓑ commit
Ⓒ landscaper Ⓓ computerize

(4) Ⓐ consider Ⓑ compromise
Ⓒ contract Ⓓ contact

(5) Ⓐ additional Ⓑ addition
Ⓒ in addition to Ⓓ in addition

第十八組中文翻譯與解答解析

致：所有員工

來自：辦公室經理Sharon Lee

我寄這封信提醒大家，我們的部門預定下星期四早上九點要開會，以下是議程大綱：

早上十點	介紹新進員工
早上十點十五分	複習上次會議紀錄
早上十點三十分	當季報告
早上十點五十分	策略計畫：3H公司的合併案
早上十一點三十分	組織企劃委員會
中午十二點	會議結束

假如你還有另外的議程，請在週二下午五點前聯絡我，我會在週三下午傳送一份確定的議程表。

(1) Ⓐ draft（草案 n.） Ⓑ drafting（製圖 n.）
Ⓒ drafty（通風良好的 adj.） Ⓓ daft（愚笨的 adj.）
解 Ⓐ（draft 草案。）

(2) Ⓐ introduce（介紹 v.） Ⓑ introduction（介紹 n.）
Ⓒ interact（互動 v.） Ⓓ interaction（互動 n.）
解 Ⓑ（introduction 介紹*名詞用法。）

(3) Ⓐ committee（委員會 n.） Ⓑ commit（承諾 v.）
Ⓒ landscaper（園藝者 n.） Ⓓ computerize（電腦化 v.）
解 Ⓐ（committe 委員會。）

(4) Ⓐ consider（考慮 v.） Ⓑ compromise（妥協 v.）
Ⓒ contract（合約 n.） Ⓓ contact（聯絡 v.）
解 Ⓓ（contact 聯絡。）

(5) Ⓐ additional（額外的adj.） Ⓑ addition（附加 n.）
Ⓒ in addition to（除此之外 ） Ⓓ in addition（另外）
解 Ⓐ（additional 附加的*形容詞用法。）

第十九組題目

Hi, Tom, I know we had planned to go out to dinner tonight, but I'm afraid that something has just come over and I have to ___(1)___ our date. My cat ___(2)___ by a dog today and I'm very upset about it because the cat was a gift from my parents. I still cannot recover from the shock of my cat's frightening ___(3)___. I'm really sorry about this, especially because it's the third time I've cancelled on you this month. I'm not sure when I'll be ___(4)___, but I'll definitely call you. Thanks for your ___(5)___. Bye for now.

(1) Ⓐ call for　Ⓑ call off
Ⓒ call up　Ⓓ call in

(2) Ⓐ was bitten　Ⓑ bit
Ⓒ had bitten　Ⓓ was biting

(3) Ⓐ expense　Ⓑ experiment
Ⓒ expiration　Ⓓ experience

(4) Ⓐ vacant　Ⓑ available
Ⓒ acceptable　Ⓓ avoidable

(5) Ⓐ understandable　Ⓑ understanding
Ⓒ understood　Ⓓ understooding

第十九組中文翻譯與解答解析

嗨！湯姆，我知道我們約好今天晚上要出去吃飯，但是我恐怕有點事情，必須要取消約會。我的貓今天被狗咬了，我很不開心，因為那隻貓是我父母送我的，我還不能夠從我的小貓的可怕經驗衝擊當中平復過來。我真的很抱歉，尤其因為這是這個月第三次取消我們的約定，我不確定我什麼時候會有空，但是我一定會打電話給你。謝謝你的諒解，拜拜。

---

(1) Ⓐ call for（要求 v.）　Ⓑ call off（取消 v.）
Ⓒ call up（打電話 v.）　Ⓓ call in（招集 v.）
解 Ⓑ（call off 取消*動詞用法。）

(2) Ⓐ was bitten　Ⓑ bit
Ⓒ had bitten　Ⓓ was biting
解 Ⓐ（was bitten 被動語態。）

(3) Ⓐ expense（費用 n.）　Ⓑ experiment（實驗 n.）
Ⓒ expiration（到期 n.）　Ⓓ experience（經驗 n.）
解 Ⓓ（experience 經驗*名詞用法。）

(4) Ⓐ vacant（空的 adj.）　Ⓑ available（有空的 adj.）
Ⓒ acceptable（可接受的 adj.）　Ⓓ avoidable（可避免的adj.）
解 Ⓑ（available 有空的*形容詞用法。）

(5) Ⓐ understandable　Ⓑ understanding
Ⓒ understood　Ⓓ understooding
解 Ⓑ（understanding 理解*名詞用法。）

第二十組題目

I've always wanted to hang around by myself in Taipei City. As I'm especially interested ___(1)___ visiting some historic sites or old temples, some friends of mine suggest that there ___(2)___ one that is a must. They say that for a chance to ___(3)___ through a Taoist temple over a hundred years old, you should visit Chihnan Temple. To reach the temple you have to travel outside the city to the hills of Mucha. Then you walk up 200 or more stone ___(4)___. Don't worry, though, the views from the top are definitely ___(5)___ the effort.

(1) Ⓐ at　Ⓑ of　Ⓒ in　Ⓓ on

(2) Ⓐ is　Ⓑ be　Ⓒ are　Ⓓ will be

(3) Ⓐ wander　Ⓑ wandering　Ⓒ wonder　Ⓓ wind

(4) Ⓐ steps　Ⓑ elevators　Ⓒ processes　Ⓓ ways

(5) Ⓐ worthy　Ⓑ worth　Ⓒ worthless　Ⓓ weary

第二十組中文翻譯與解答解析

一直以來，我想要一個人在臺北逛逛。因為我對於參訪歷史景點或是老舊的廟宇特別有興趣，所以我的一些朋友建議有一間廟我一定要去。他們說如果你想要到有百年以上歷史的道教廟宇走走，你應該要到指南宮參觀。想要探訪這間廟宇，你必須要走出市區，到木柵的山坡地，然後你必須要攀登二百個以上的石階。不過別擔心，山頂上的風景絕對值得你費這番功夫上山。

---

(1) Ⓐ at　Ⓑ of
Ⓒ in　Ⓓ on
解 Ⓒ（interested in 對……有興趣。）

(2) Ⓐ is　Ⓑ be
Ⓒ are　Ⓓ will be
解 Ⓑ（suggest 的句型，suggest that S + 可以省略的 should+V 原形，故本句可以寫成 suggest that there should be one that is a must 或是suggest that there be one that is a must。）

(3) Ⓐ wander（漫遊 v.）　Ⓑ wandering（wander 的動名詞）
Ⓒ wonder（想知道 v.）　Ⓓ wind（風 n.）
解 Ⓐ（wander 徘徊。）

(4) Ⓐ steps（階梯 n.）　Ⓑ elevators（電梯 n.）
Ⓒ processes（過程 n.）　Ⓓ ways（方式 n.）
解 Ⓐ（階梯。）

(5) Ⓐ worthy（有價值的 adj.）　Ⓑ worth（有……價值的 adj.）
(C) worthless（無價值的 adj.）　(D) weary（疲倦的 adj.）
解 Ⓑ（be + worth 是值得的。）

Chapter 4

段落填空題型模擬試題二十組

良好的閱讀習慣應該還包括多閱讀各式各樣不同的文體與主題，例如文章的文體包括有議論文（argumentation）、描寫文（description）、說明文（exposition）、敘述文（narration）等，除了這四類文體之外，一般書信、商業書信、公告、告示牌、電話留言、廣告、菜單、宣傳單等都是可以注意的閱讀內容。同時，千萬不要拘泥在一種主題上打轉，例如對歷史主題有興趣者，也應多閱讀生物化學等主題，對於企業管理主題有興趣者也應多看看政治或是文化方面的主題，也就是各式的主題均應有所涉獵。以下提供二十組的段落填空練習，題材皆多樣化。

第一組

One day, there was a hungry fox looking for something to eat. He saw a crow ___(1)___ up into a tree. The crow had a piece of meat in her mouth. The fox wanted the meat for ___(2)___ because he was really starving. He had an idea ___(3)___ he thought a minute. He said to the crow," Oh, dear crow, how beautiful you are! With shining feathers and bright eyes, your voice ___(4)___ be beautiful, too." The crow was so ___(5)___ that she began to sing, and certainly, the meat fell out of the crow's mouth and became the fox's lunch. The crow shouted, "You thief, you stole my meat, didn't you?" The fox then said to the crow, "Yes, I did. And remember not to believe someone who says too many good things on you!"

(1) Ⓐ flew Ⓑ to fly
Ⓒ fly Ⓓ has flown

(2) Ⓐ himself Ⓑ him
Ⓒ it Ⓓ myself

(3) Ⓐ before Ⓑ after
Ⓒ as long as Ⓓ since

(4) Ⓐ maybe Ⓑ has to
Ⓒ must Ⓓ probably

(5) Ⓐ worried Ⓑ shame
Ⓒ proud Ⓓ clever

第二組

Online chatting has become one of the most popular activities for everybody. You can make new friends easily at home, and you don't need to go out to meet one. You can see many teenagers ___(1)___ their computer at home without leaving their rooms. With a computer, chatting with somebody far away is not a very difficult thing. That is also the reason why I always stay at home by ___(2)___ using my computer day and night.

To tell the truth, I don't think that it's safe to tell anything detailed when chatting online. Therefore, don't give your real name, telephone number, ___(3)___ home address. If you tell everything about yourself when chatting, you ___(4)___ get into a big trouble. Just keep in mind that ___(5)___ is the best policy!

---

(1) Ⓐ typed Ⓑ to type
Ⓒ type Ⓓ has typed

(2) Ⓐ myself Ⓑ me
Ⓒ it Ⓓ himself

(3) Ⓐ also Ⓑ or
Ⓒ but Ⓓ as

(4) Ⓐ maybe Ⓑ might be
Ⓒ may Ⓓ lovely

(5) Ⓐ crew Ⓑ knowledge
Ⓒ safety Ⓓ management

第三組

David found a puppy on his way home from work yesterday. ___(1)___ so weak and helpless. He has ___(2)___ wanted to have a pet; therefore, he decided to keep it right at that moment. Now the only problem he concerns is that his wife is allergic to hairy animals. In order to solve this problem, David is going to make a dog house outside and ___(3)___ the puppy in the front yard.

David also decided to ask his best friend Bob, who has kept a dog for many years, about some ___(4)___ for raising a pet. Actually, Bob was very helpful when David talked to him. He told David some useful information, including how much he should feed the dog, how to wash it and play with it as well as make it happy. ___(5)___, he also reminded David to take his puppy to see a vet regularly for its health.

---

(1) Ⓐ Its Ⓑ It was
Ⓒ They were Ⓓ They

(2) Ⓐ always Ⓑ usual
Ⓒ never Ⓓ not often

(3) Ⓐ kept Ⓑ keep
Ⓒ keeping Ⓓ to keeping

(4) Ⓐ tips Ⓑ tapes
Ⓒ times Ⓓ cases

(5) Ⓐ However Ⓑ In other words
Ⓒ Besides Ⓓ As a result

第四組

A lot of people like to take a long walk in the park in an early morning. At this time of the day, the fresh air can help ___(1)___ them up. According to some reports done by some well-known experts, people who ___(2)___ to take an early morning walk think this type of ___(3)___ makes them become healthier.

As a matter of fact, people of all ages can enjoy walking. When they walk in the park, they can watch some beautiful flowers and tall trees around them, and leave their worries on the grass. They are always full of energy ___(4)___ they try to start their day in this way. They also feel happy after they finish this long walk. Take me ___(5)___, whenever I feel particularly stressed, I always walk in the park near my home for some time. There, I can watch people doing many different activities and forget something bad easily. That's so much fun.

---

(1) Ⓐ stand　Ⓑ give
　Ⓒ wake　Ⓓ wipe

(2) Ⓐ love　Ⓑ loving
　Ⓒ loved　Ⓓ are love

(3) Ⓐ weather　Ⓑ exercise
　Ⓒ park　Ⓓ refreshment

(4) Ⓐ where　Ⓑ unless
　Ⓒ if　Ⓓ as soon as

(5) Ⓐ like case　Ⓑ as an example
　Ⓒ for example　Ⓓ as if an example

第五組

Camping is a great way to spend your vacation. First of all, it doesn't cost much money. Without paying a lot for a hotel, you can stay at a ___(1)___ in the beautiful park and sleep in the tent. Have you ever slept under the stars? That's really amazing! Also, cooking over a campfire ___(2)___ a lot of fun. Believe me, food cooked over a campfire can always make your mouth water.

I know ___(3)___ someone will concern about the safety, but in my opinion, people of all ages can enjoy camping ___(4)___ they give it a try. The best thing is that you can have some happy hours with your family and ___(5)___ and leave your worries there. It'll sure be an unforgettable experience!

---

(1) Ⓐ barn　Ⓑ campsite
　Ⓒ motel　Ⓓ bench

(2) Ⓐ is　Ⓑ does
　Ⓒ are　Ⓓ do

(3) Ⓐ may　Ⓑ maybe
　Ⓒ may be　Ⓓ might

(4) Ⓐ once　Ⓑ unless
　Ⓒ while　Ⓓ even though

(5) Ⓐ relation　Ⓑ relationship
　Ⓒ relatives　Ⓓ related

第六組

A long time ago, going to a dentist could be a terrible thing because there was no medicine ease the pain when you have your tooth ___(1)___ out. Then a young dentist named Milton wanted to solve this problem. Firstly, he tried to use gas to make animals sleep. After several tests, he decided to use gas to make people sleep, and it worked ___(2)___. While the patients ___(3)___, Milton tried to pull out their teeth, and ___(4)___ didn't feel any pain. As a result, Milton became a very famous dentist at that time. He was so well-known that he had lots of patients to take care. Since then, gas has become a necessary and important tool ___(5)___ doctors do operations.

(1) Ⓐ pull Ⓑ to pull
Ⓒ pulled Ⓓ pulling

(2) Ⓐ amazingly Ⓑ terribly
Ⓒ roughly Ⓓ unfortunately

(3) Ⓐ sleep Ⓑ were sleeping
Ⓒ have slept Ⓓ are sleeping

(4) Ⓐ he Ⓑ you
Ⓒ they Ⓓ it

(5) Ⓐ until Ⓑ after
Ⓒ when Ⓓ because

第七組

Many people have learned English for a long time, and English has become the most important thing in their daily life. They can talk to some foreigners easily when they travel in English speaking countries. ___(1)___, they still think writing English essays is a hard task. In fact, many people still are afraid of writing in English. One great way to improve writing skill is just to read in English a lot. ___(2)___ will help you become more familiar with common grammar and ___(3)___ your vocabulary. Writing is always easier when you know a lot of vocabulary. The other thing that it is necessary to do is to write! " Practice makes perfect," ___(4)___ they say. ___(5)___ a regular writing time for yourself by taking a class, picking up a writing workbook or just trying to exchange English e-mails with friends. Following the steps, you will be a good English writer in the near future!

---

(1) Ⓐ In addition to Ⓑ However
Ⓒ Thus Ⓓ In other words

(2) Ⓐ They Ⓑ Its
Ⓒ This Ⓓ Those

(3) Ⓐ decline Ⓑ refuse
Ⓒ rise Ⓓ increase

(4) Ⓐ for Ⓑ as if
Ⓒ likewise Ⓓ as

(5) Ⓐ Create Ⓑ Creating
Ⓒ Created Ⓓ To create

第八組

To: All employees

From: HR Office

Subject: Safety Regulation Training

Starting from next month, all employees are required to complete a training course on the safety ___(1)___ in effect at our different sites. The course is self-contained; ___(2)___, you can take the course at any time at your convenience. The Learning Center is open from 8:30 AM to 8:00 PM, except for the lunch time. Thanks to the interactive CD-ROMs, you ___(3)___ learn at your own pace with the training materials. A printout at the end of the training session will give you the results. Remember that everyone has to get it done before the deadline May 20th .The will be no other opportunity to have the training course ___(4)___ next year at this time.

(1) Ⓐ amendments Ⓑ alumni
Ⓒ extravagance Ⓓ procedures

(2) Ⓐ nevertheless Ⓑ as a consequence
Ⓒ to sum up Ⓓ on the other hand

(3) Ⓐ can be able to Ⓑ will be able to
Ⓒ will can Ⓓ will have able to

(4) Ⓐ no matter how Ⓑ when
Ⓒ as long as Ⓓ till

第九組

Lots of people study English for ages and become functional in their daily life. They can survive talking to the occasional foreigners or get around with ease when they travel in other countries. However, still many people tend to struggle in their attempt to write clearly in English. This is where gaps in grammar comprehension and spelling ___(1)___ glaringly obvious. One great way to improve writing skill doesn't even involve holding a pen. It is enormously helpful to just read in English. This will help you become more familiar with common grammar structures and increase your vocabulary. It will also expose you to the spelling of ___(2)___ that you may know to hear, but not to see. Writing is always easier when you have a model to on which to draw. The other thing is essential to do is to write, write and write! Practice makes perfect, as they say. Create a regular writing time for yourself ___(3)___ taking a class, picking up a writing workbook or just trying to exchange English e-mail with some friends, your classmates, or colleagues. Practice explaining things or describing a scene you see at once. Then give your work to someone and ask for his or her opinion. Don't be afraid of ___(4)___. Having other people point out your weak areas is necessary if you want to correct problems. Are you ready? Let's get it started.

---

(1) Ⓐ become Ⓑ remain Ⓒ interfere Ⓓ remunerate

(2) Ⓐ vocabularies Ⓑ words Ⓒ alphabets Ⓓ liters

(3) Ⓐ instead of Ⓑ by Ⓒ with Ⓓ in spite of

(4) Ⓐ critics Ⓑ critiques Ⓒ criticism Ⓓ critters

第十組

Dear customers,

Starting from next month, we will no longer be accepting Chad' Café Coupons. The recent ___(1)___ price of coffee beans has made it difficult to keep ___(2)___.

The everyday low prices that our customers have come ___(3)___ and the high quality of our drinks. We have decided not to raise prices. We still would like to let our customers pleased with our prices. As a consequence, we will ___(4)___ the coupon system. We will accept coupons till the end of the month.

Thanks very much for your understanding.

Chad's Coffee Shop

---

(1) Ⓐ increase　Ⓑ increasing
　Ⓒ include　Ⓓ including

(2) Ⓐ both　Ⓑ neither
　Ⓒ either　Ⓓ as well as

(3) Ⓐ to expect　Ⓑ expect
　Ⓒ expecting　Ⓓ except

(4) Ⓐ do away with　Ⓑ keep in touch with
　Ⓒ look up to　Ⓓ have nothing to do with

第十一組

As we enter the flu season, the top management team wants to remind all employees ___(1)___ their hands after ___(2)___ the restroom and returning back to work.

This is especially important for our servers. As you know, germs, viruses, ___(3)___ are passed on through hand contact. Here at Charles' good restaurant, hygiene and ___(4)___ are our number one priorities. This policy will be strictly enforced. Thanks very much for your cooperation.

The management

(1) Ⓐ wash Ⓑ to wash Ⓒ washing Ⓓ washed

(2) Ⓐ use Ⓑ to use Ⓒ using Ⓓ used

(3) Ⓐ bacteria Ⓑ bacterial Ⓒ bacteriology Ⓓ bacteries

(4) Ⓐ clean Ⓑ cleanliness Ⓒ cleaness Ⓓ cleanly

第十二組

This notice is ___(1)___ you of the following situation. Two weeks ago, the office caught some students ___(2)___ exams. They were using their portable phones to text message answers to other students. I want all teachers to pay more attention to students' behavior during the exams. Cheating will not be ___(3)___. If students cheat on exams, they will get an F and two-day ___(4)___ from school. Thanks for your help in this matter.

Principal Charles Chen

---

1. Ⓐ inform Ⓑ to inform
   Ⓒ informing Ⓓ informed
2. Ⓐ cheated on Ⓑ be cheated on
   Ⓒ cheating on Ⓓ are cheating on
3. Ⓐ tolerated Ⓑ tolerate
   Ⓒ toleration Ⓓ tolerating
4. Ⓐ suspension Ⓑ stay
   Ⓒ layoff Ⓓ dismissal

第十三組

May 6th 1993

Dear Chairman Wang,

I have been ___(1)___ with the relations between our company and yours during the last ten years. I am also very much pleased to learn that you are coming to visit here in Taipei during our Chinese New Year period and will stay for one week. If it proved convenient to you, may we ___(2)___ you in my head office at 5:00 PM on January 25th, 2009. A dinner in your honor will follow our meeting. ___(3)___ special persons or institutes in mind which you want us to make arrangements for you, please do not hesitate to let me know. Thanks so much for continuing the warm ___(4)___ that exists between our two companies. This time, I would like you have a wonderful vacation as well as a successful meeting here in Taipei.

Sincerely yours,

Chad Chen

---

(1) Ⓐ delighted　Ⓑ dreary
　Ⓒ dismal　Ⓓ cheerless

(2) Ⓐ anticipate　Ⓑ look for
　Ⓒ give　Ⓓ participate in

(3) Ⓐ If you had　Ⓑ Should you have
　Ⓒ In case of you have　Ⓓ If you should have to

(4) Ⓐ endowment　Ⓑ discrepancy
　Ⓒ hospitality　Ⓓ disputes

第十四組

Billy,

I know we had planned to go out to dinner tonight, but I'm afraid that something has just come ___(1)___ and I have to cancel our date. My sister's cat ___(2)___ by my dog today and she's very upset about it because the cat was a gift from her boyfriend. She called me in tears a few minutes ago and asked if I could stay with her tonight ___(3)___ she recovers from the shock of her cat's frightening ___(4)___. I'm so sorry about this. I'm not sure when I'll be available, but I'll definitely call you when I am free. Thanks for ___(5)___ understanding.

Love, Nadia

---

(1) Ⓐ under Ⓑ over Ⓒ with Ⓓ on

(2) Ⓐ was bitten Ⓑ bit Ⓒ had bitten Ⓓ was biting

(3) Ⓐ when Ⓑ during Ⓒ until Ⓓ since

(4) Ⓐ expense Ⓑ experiment Ⓒ expiration Ⓓ experience

(5) Ⓐ you Ⓑyour Ⓒ yours Ⓓ yourself

第十五組

Last year I had the wonderful experience in the USA. I attended the wedding of my friends from the community college. The bride and the groom were all my classmates in the same class. Let me __(1)__ what happened on the wedding day. First, the guests arrived at the church. When everybody was __(2)__, the groom and his best man entered the church and stood in front. Then, a musician group began to play the "Wedding March", and the bridesmaids began to march slowly down the aisle. Finally, the bride __(3)__ and walked down the aisle beside her father. __(4)__ the ceremony, the groom gave the bride a wedding ring. After they kissed each other, they left the church arm in arm. Every moment was so beautiful and extremely exciting.

After the ceremony, there was a wedding __(5)__. I didn't attend the reception, but I heard everyone had a wonderful time. I enjoyed the process of a traditional American wedding so much. Even right now, when I think about this special experience, I always wear a smile on my face. That's indeed a sweet memory.

---

(1) Ⓐ assist Ⓑ subscribe Ⓒ narrate Ⓓ utilize

(2) Ⓐ sat Ⓑ seated Ⓒ sit Ⓓ seat

(3) Ⓐ had appeared Ⓑ appearing Ⓒ appeared Ⓓ appear

(4) Ⓐ During Ⓑ By the time Ⓒ While Ⓓ Until

(5) Ⓐ rejection Ⓑ recipe Ⓒ receipt Ⓓ reception

第十六組

Dear Mr. Smith,

Thank you so much for your letter of August 29, 2012. I am so pleased to learn that you are coming to visit Taiwan and will stay here for one week. According ___(1)___ the letter I received from you, we will expect you in Taipei office of our company at 10:00AM on September 9, 2012. ___(2)___ let you know more about our operations here, I've arranged a presentation at our main office for you. I ___(3)___ you some information about future developments in our company. A welcome lunch in your honor will follow our presentation. ___(4)___ you have some special persons and institutions in mind that you wish us to make arrangements for you, please feel free to tell me.

I am proud of the good relations between our two companies, and I ___(5)___ believe that your visit in September will be a great success. I am looking forward to seeing you soon.

Best regards,

Helen Wu

---

(1) Ⓐ with Ⓑ by Ⓒ to Ⓓ on

(2) Ⓐ In order that Ⓑ In order to
Ⓒ So that Ⓓ As so to

(3) Ⓐ will provide Ⓑ will be provide
Ⓒ am going to be provided Ⓓ provided

(4) Ⓐ Even though Ⓑ Seeing that
Ⓒ If Ⓓ Unless

(5) Ⓐ strongly Ⓑ presently
Ⓒ previously Ⓓ obviously

第十七組

To learn with success is a difficult ___(1)___. I think some fundamental principles have to be observed, and then successful learning can be achieved. Among these, ___(2)___, are diligence and devotion. First of all, all things can be done through diligent efforts. Like language learning, we always need to study hard and we can ___(3)___ the language we learn. People say that a diligent fool will accomplish more than a lazy wit. Second, devotion helps us to set our mind on one thing at a time. People who like to change what they learn often can't make success a certainty. They don't know how to focus on one thing and learn things without efficiency.

To be honest, I am a person ___(4)___ always keeps these principles in my mind when learning. I am not only industrious but also devoted. Therefore, I can learn new things very quickly. For example, I am learning cooking these days in order to get my cook's certificate. To learn it successfully, I practice ___(5)___ every day, and I always pay full attention to what my instructor teaches me in class. I believe I can cook many tasty dishes in the near future.

(1) Ⓐ principal Ⓑ task Ⓒ arrangement Ⓓ dispensary

(2) Ⓐ in my opinion Ⓑ master
Ⓒ in addition Ⓓ on the other hand

(3) Ⓐ describe Ⓑ thanks to
Ⓒ transmit Ⓓ evolve

(4) Ⓐ who Ⓑ whom
Ⓒ whose Ⓓ which

(5) Ⓐ cooking Ⓑ cook
Ⓒ to cook Ⓓ cooker

第十八組

I will always remember that raw winter. It was a harsh and icy winter, but everyone in my family all ___(1)___ warm. Mr. Chang is my best friend's father. A few years ago, he was very ill because he had a heart disease. His doctor told him that he needed a new heart, and that was the only way to save his life. However, the list of people needing a new heart ___(2)___ very long. Mr. Chang once told us, "I would be a better father and cherish my family members more if I ___(3)___ this time."

Besides me, everyone in my family prayed for Mr. Chang every day. ___(4)___, a man who died because of his death penalty donated his heart and other organs. After the operation, it took Mr. Chang several months ___(5)___ his heath. After his recovery, he decided to accompany with his family more. The other day I met him, and he told me, " The heart is a gift, and now I will be devoted to my family forever, just like a gift for my family."

---

(1) Ⓐ feel　　Ⓑ felt
　Ⓒ had felt　　Ⓓ has been feeling

(2) Ⓐ were　　Ⓑ was
　Ⓒ have been　　Ⓓ being

(3) Ⓐ had better live　　Ⓑ could live
　Ⓒ ought to have lived　　Ⓓ could be lived

(4) Ⓐ Fortunately　　Ⓑ Unluckily
　Ⓒ Consequently　　Ⓓ Hesitatingly

(5) Ⓐ regain　　Ⓑ regaining
　Ⓒ regained　　Ⓓ to regain

第十九組

An interesting festival in Japan is Shichi-go-san. Shichi-go-san means "seven five three" because it is the festival ___(1)___ children who turn seven, five, and three years of age. Japanese people celebrate this festival on November 15th every year. There are some customs to follow on this festival. ___(2)___, on this day, a young girl at the age of seven, has to wear an obi around her waist with the kimono ___(3)___ public. How about five and three? A boy at the age of five has to wear his first hakama plants in public. The age of three is also imperative ___(4)___ children are allowed to let their hair ___(5)___ at three. Next time, supposed you happen to go to Japan on November 15th, take a look at some children around you, and you will know how old they are.

---

(1) Ⓐ celebrate Ⓑ celebrated
Ⓒ celebration Ⓓ celebrating

(2) Ⓐ Moreover Ⓑ In addition to
Ⓒ For instance Ⓓ Instead

(3) Ⓐ in Ⓑ on
Ⓒ by Ⓓ of

(4) Ⓐ due to the fact that Ⓑ even though
Ⓒ in the event that Ⓓ whether or not

(5) Ⓐ growing Ⓑ to grow
Ⓒ grown Ⓓ grow

第二十組

In most of the world, Beckham is a major celebrity, who ___(1)___ be on any list of the best well-known athletes. He is a soccer superstar and one of the best English soccer players of all time. Beckham was born in 1975 in England. He joined the team of Manchester United and won the Professional Football Association (PFA) Young Player of the year award in 1997. As a midfielder, Beckham helped his team win many ___(2)___ because of his skillful passing and free kicks.

Not only is he a famous athlete, but he is also a fashionable celebrity. He often shows up wearing a special hairstyle, and very soon, the new style ___(3)___. Everyone wants to have the same haircut just like Beckham. In 1999, he married a beautiful singer named Victoria Adams, who ___(4)___ also a renowned member of the popular group the Spice Girls. Now they have two sons. ___(5)___ of them are as "cute" as their father, David Beckham.

(1) Ⓐ ought Ⓑ should
Ⓒ used to Ⓓ supposed to

(2) Ⓐ championships Ⓑ events
Ⓒ defeat Ⓓ success

(3) Ⓐ caught on Ⓑ catches on
Ⓒ catching on Ⓓ is caught on

(4) Ⓐ was Ⓑ will be
Ⓒ are Ⓓ were

(5) Ⓐ Either Ⓑ Each
Ⓒ Some Ⓓ Both

段落填空題型二十組解答

第一組				
(1)	(2)	(3)	(4)	(5)
Ⓒ	Ⓐ	Ⓑ	Ⓒ	Ⓒ
第二組				
(1)	(2)	(3)	(4)	(5)
Ⓒ	Ⓐ	Ⓑ	Ⓒ	Ⓒ
第三組				
(1)	(2)	(3)	(4)	(5)
Ⓑ	Ⓐ	Ⓑ	Ⓐ	Ⓒ
第四組				
(1)	(2)	(3)	(4)	(5)
Ⓒ	Ⓐ	Ⓑ	Ⓓ	Ⓒ
第五組				
(1)	(2)	(3)	(4)	(5)
Ⓑ	Ⓐ	Ⓑ	Ⓐ	Ⓒ
第六組				
(1)	(2)	(3)	(4)	(5)
Ⓒ	Ⓐ	Ⓑ	Ⓒ	Ⓒ
第七組				
(1)	(2)	(3)	(4)	(5)
Ⓑ	Ⓒ	Ⓓ	Ⓓ	Ⓐ
第八組				
(1)	(2)	(3)	(4)	
Ⓓ	Ⓑ	Ⓑ	Ⓓ	
第九組				
(1)	(2)	(3)	(4)	
Ⓐ	Ⓑ	Ⓑ	Ⓒ	

第十組				
(1)	(2)	(3)	(4)	
Ⓑ	Ⓐ	Ⓐ	Ⓐ	

第十一組				
(1)	(2)	(3)	(4)	
Ⓑ	Ⓒ	Ⓐ	Ⓑ	

第十二組				
(1)	(2)	(3)	(4)	
Ⓑ	Ⓒ	Ⓐ	Ⓐ	

第十三組				
(1)	(2)	(3)	(4)	
Ⓐ	Ⓐ	Ⓑ	Ⓒ	

第十四組				
(1)	(2)	(3)	(4)	(5)
Ⓑ	Ⓐ	Ⓒ	Ⓓ	Ⓑ

第十五組				
(1)	(2)	(3)	(4)	(5)
Ⓒ	Ⓑ	Ⓒ	Ⓐ	Ⓓ

第十六組				
(1)	(2)	(3)	(4)	(5)
Ⓒ	Ⓑ	Ⓐ	Ⓒ	Ⓐ

第十七組				
(1)	(2)	(3)	(4)	(5)
Ⓑ	Ⓐ	Ⓑ	Ⓐ	Ⓐ

第十八組				
(1)	(2)	(3)	(4)	(5)
Ⓑ	Ⓑ	Ⓑ	Ⓐ	Ⓓ

第十九組				
(1)	(2)	(3)	(4)	(5)
Ⓓ	Ⓒ	Ⓐ	Ⓐ	Ⓓ
第二十組				
(1)	(2)	(3)	(4)	(5)
Ⓑ	Ⓐ	Ⓑ	Ⓐ	Ⓓ

Chapter 5

閱讀理解題型題目介紹

現在很多的英文考試內容越來越符合實用化及生活化的原則，舉凡路標、交通標誌、招牌、廣告、時刻表、菜單、食譜、卡通、賀卡、便條、故事、表格、私人信件等，都可成為考試的題材，考生平時宜多留意這一類生活相關事物的英文用語，譬如到西餐廳用餐時，注意菜單上的英文用詞，有空時買份英文報紙，看看其分類廣告、電視節目表的寫法。在考試時閱讀的目的是答對試題冊上的問題，因此閱讀文章前先很快地看一次文章後的題目，可以幫助建立閱讀該文的目標，引導閱讀的方向，從而提高閱讀的速度。以下十一組多樣化的題型設計為範例。

第一組題目（問候卡）

Dear May,

Get well soon! We all miss you very much!

Your best friend

Kim

Best Wishes

1. Why did Kim write the card to May?

   (A) Because May is feeling sad and unhappy.

   (B) Because May is sick.

   (C) Because May has finished school.

   (D) Because it's May's birthday.

2. What's the relationship between May and Kim?

   (A) Coworker (B) Sibling

   (C) Classmate (D) Friend

第二組題目（索引）

INDEX

TITLE	PAGE	COPYRIGHT
Business Laws	57	1983
How to have a promotion	88	1987
Be successful at your workplace	90	2003
Communication with your boss	190	1999

1. Who would most likely use this index?

(A) Lawyer (B) Marketing expert

(C) Business people (D) Teacher

2. Which book has the most recent copyright?

(A) Business Laws

(B) How to have a promotion

(C) Be successful at your workplace

(D) Communication with your boss

第三組題目（邀請函）

Birthday Party Invitation

At May's house(18923 Broke Road)

Saturday, June 13th , 7:00PM

Please ASAP 234-7856

(We have drinks and various foods)

1. When is the party?

(A) May (B) June

(C) Sunday (D) April

2. What should the receiver do?

(A) Call back (B) Send an email

(C) Send an invitation (D) Order some food

第四組題目（販售廣告）

WEEKEND SALES

Office Furniture offers you the lowest prices in town!!

All desks and chairs——40% off

All sofas——half price

No delivery.

On Maple Avenue.

Across from CITY HALL.

1. How long is the sale?

   (A) All weekdays　　(B) 5 days

   (C) 2 days　　(D) 40 days

2. Where is Office Furniture?

   (A) On Main Avenue　　(B) Across from City Bank

   (C) In City Hall　　(D) Near City Hall

第五組題目（徵才廣告）

WANTED

System Computer is seeking an office manager. Applicants must have a master's degree and at least 6 years' experience. Can speak English well. Have to work overtime if there is a need. Interested one please prepares a resume. IN PERSON. We don't accept mail or fax.

1. Which of the following is the job announcement for?

   (A) An office assistant　　(B) A computer programmer

   (C) An English teacher　　(D) A manager

2. Which of the following must applicants have?

(A) Can speak English well.
(B) Have a doctor's degree.
(C) Have 10 years' experience.
(D) Have a computer.

3. How can applicants apply for the job?

(A) Call
(B) In person
(C) Fax
(D) Mail

第六組題目（行事曆）

APPOINTMENT CALENDAR by Bill

Mar. 30 Mon.	Meet manager at the main office at 8:30 a.m. Give a report at 9:00a.m.
Mar. 31 Tue.	7:00 p.m. visit some clients 8:00 p.m. buy a birthday gift for my lovely daughter
Apr. 1 Wed.	12:00 p.m. Lunch at Anna' Café w / Andrea 4:00 p.m. Meet with new coworkers

1. What schedule does this appointment calendar show?

(A) A work week only
(B) Monday to Wednesday
(C) March 30 to April 5
(D) All weekend

2. What can we know from this calendar?

(A) Bill has a lovely son.
(B) It will not be longer than a half hour to meet the manager.
(C) Bill has to work overtime.
(D) Bill will visit some clients on April 1st.

3. Who is Bill seeing on Wednesday?

(A) Charlie
(B) Anna
(C) John
(D) Andrea

第七組題目（感謝卡）

Dear Miss Smith:

I'm so happy to be your student.

May you have a wonderful holiday and the best blessings in the coming year.

Jane

1. On which holiday did Jane send the card?

   (A) On Valentine's Day. (B) On the Easter.

   (C) On New Year's Day. (D) On Halloween.

2. Who will Jane send this card to?

   (A) Her mother (B) Her teacher

   (C) Her colleague (D) Her former boss

第八組題目（電話留言）

TO: Mr. Muro

Date: 8 / 21

Time: 3:08 P.M. (while you were out)

Caller:

Mr. / Ms. Tom Keng

Of Pacific Telecompany

Phone:(253) 555-6736 ext. 432

(√) PLEASE CALL ( ) WILL CALL BACK

Messages: Today's meeting has been cancelled.

Mr. JC rearranged the time to next Monday.

Operator

Miss Li

1. Who made the phone call?

(A) Miss Li (B) Tom Keng

(C) Mr. Muro (D) Mr. JC

2. Why was the call made?

(A) To call off a conference. (B) To confirm the meeting.

(C) To inform a new event. (D) To arrange a party.

第九組題目（長條圖）

The percentage of reading on different magazines

(Survey a : 2009.04~2010.03)

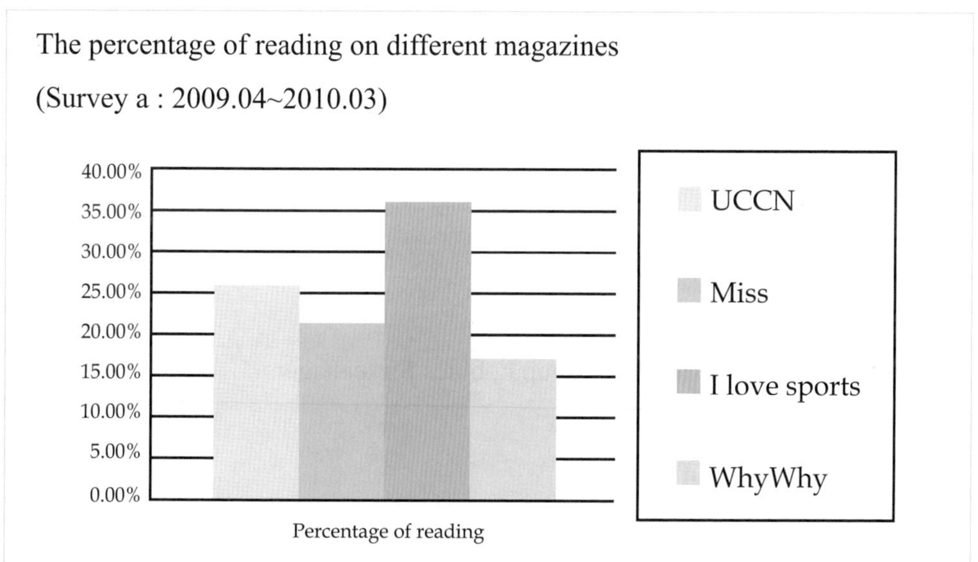

1. Which magazine has the highest percentage of reading?

(A) UCCN (B) Miss

(C) I love sports (D) WhyWhy

2. How much time does this graph cover?

(A) Half a year (B) 4 months

(C) one month (D) one year

第十組題目（問卷）

Hobby Survey for teenagers

Topic: What do you usually do in your spare time?

1. Get online 10%
2. Play PC games 15%
3. Go shopping 6%
4. Watch TV 25%
5. Study 30%
6. Go for outdoor activity 10%
7. Go for night bar or club 4%

1. What is the most uncommon hobby for teenagers?

(A) Go shopping

(B) Go for night bars or clubs

(C) Go for outdoor activity

(D) Sleep

2. What are two of the most common hobbies for teenagers?

(A) Study and watch TV

(B) Go shopping and get online

(C) Go for outdoor activity and go for night bar or club

(D) None of the above

第十一組題目（雙篇閱讀：議程與電子郵件）

Worldwide International, Inc.

Division Heads Conference

Wednesday, December 7th 3:30P.M.

Place: Company Meeting Room 5

AGENDA

1. Office supplies issues
2. Winter conference plans
3. The year-end banquet
4. New HR regulations
5. Review last year's performance
6. Budget report

To : Anita Blair

From : Jasmine Rosemary

Re: Yesterday's conference

Dear Anita,

I am concerned about your sudden illness. Are you feeling better now? The conference yesterday went well, and it started on time. We rearranged the order of the agenda a bit. We talked about the fifth item first because we all thought that the last year's performance needed a quick review, and then we can go ahead for the coming year. The meeting lasted for 2 hours and we had no extra time to finish the sixth item. We set the date for the next month's conference, which should include the item we didn't discuss this time. It will be held on the 17th. Also, because some outside consultants will participate in the next meeting, we need a bigger room to make everyone more comfortable. I think Room 5 is too small. Either Room 1 or Room 3 will be a good choice.

Cheers,

Jasmine

1. What item was discussed last?

   (A) Review last year's performance (B) New HR regulations

   (C) Office supplies issues (D) Budget report

2. What time did the meeting end?

   (A) 3:30P.M. (B) 5:30P.M.

   (C) 4:30P.M. (D) 2:30P.M.

3. Where will the next meeting be held?

   (A) Room 5 (B) Either Room 1 or 5

   (C) Either Room 1 or 3 (D) Company Cafeteria

4. When is the next meeting?

   (A) December 17th (B) January 17th

   (C) December 7th (D) January 7th

5. Why didn't they discuss one of the items?

   (A) There were some advisors'coming (B) They were lack of time

   (C) Ms. Blair was suddenly sick (D) Room 5 was too small

第一至十一組中文翻譯與解答

第一組題目（問候卡）

親愛的梅，
祝早日康復！我們都非常想念妳！
妳最好的朋友
肯

Best Wishes

1. 為何肯要寫這張卡片給梅？
   (A) 因為梅覺得傷心與難過　(B) 因為梅生病了
   (C) 因為梅畢業了　(D) 因為梅生日
2. 梅與肯的關係為何？
   (A) 同事　(B) 手足
   (C) 同學　(D) 朋友

第二組題目（索引）

索引

標題	頁數	版權
商業法規	57	1983
如何獲得升遷	88	1987
在職場上成功	90	2003
和老闆溝通	190	1999

1. 誰最有可能使用這個索引？

(A) 律師 (B) 行銷專家

(C) 商業人士 (D) 老師

2. 哪一本書的版權最新？

(A) 商業法規 (B) 如何獲得升遷

(C) 在職場上成功 (D) 和老闆溝通

第三組題目（邀請函）

Birthday Party Invitation

在梅的家（布客路 18923 號）

週六，六月十三日，晚上七點鐘

請儘快回覆 234-7856

（備有飲料與各式各樣的食物）

1. 派對是在何時？

(A) 五月 (B) 六月

(C) 週日 (D) 四月

2. 收到邀請函的人要做什麼？

(A) 回電 (B) 寄電子郵件

(C) 寄邀請函 (D) 訂購食物

第四組題目（販售廣告）

週末特賣

辦公室家具公司提供給你本地的最低優惠價！！

所有桌椅——打6折

所有沙發——半價
不予配送
位於楓葉大道
市政府對面

SALE

1. 這回的特賣持續多久？

(A) 整個週間（週一至週五）　(B) 五天

(C) 兩天　(D) 四十天

2. 辦公室家具公司位於何處？

(A) 在楓葉大道上　(B) 在市銀行對面

(C) 在市政府內　(D) 在市政府附近

第五組題目（徵才廣告）

徵人啟事

系統電腦公司徵求辦公室經理。應徵者必須具有碩士學歷且至少六年以上的工作經驗、英語流利，可以配合加班。有意者請備履歷表、親自前來申請，不接受郵件或是傳真。

1. 本則啟事徵求何種職位？

(A) 辦公室助理　(B) 電腦程式設計師

(C) 英文老師　(D) 經理

2. 應徵者必需具備下列何項資格？

(A) 英語流利　(B) 有博士學位

(C) 有十年的工作經驗　(D) 有一台電腦

3. 應徵者要如何申請這份工作？

(A) 打電話　(B) 親自前往

(C) 傳真　(D) 郵寄

第六組題目（行事曆）

比爾的行事曆

三月三十日 週一	上午八點三十分與經理在大辦公室會晤 上午九點發表報告
三月三十一日 週二	晚上七點拜訪客戶 晚上八點買心愛女兒的生日禮物
四月一日 週三	中午十二點與安迪亞在安娜咖啡館吃午餐 下午四點鐘會見新進同事

1. 此行事曆顯示什麼行程？

(A) 一個工作週　(B) 週一到週三

(C) 三月三十日到四月五日　(D) 整個週末

2. 從行程中我們可以得知何事？

(A) 比爾有一個可愛的兒子

(B) 與經理的會面不會超過半小時

(C) 比爾必須要加班

(D) 比爾在四月一日要拜訪一些顧客

3. 比爾在週三要與誰見面？

(A) Charlie　(B) Anna

(C) John　(D) Andrea

第七組題目（感謝卡）

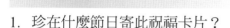

親愛的史密斯小姐：

我真的很開心可以成為你的學生。

願你有個很棒的假期並在未來的新年獻上我誠摯的祝福！

珍

1. 珍在什麼節日寄此祝福卡片？

(A) 情人節　　(B) 復活節

(C) 新年　　(D) 萬聖節

2. 珍將這張卡片寄給誰？

(A) 她的母親　　(B) 她的老師

(C) 她的同事　　(D) 她的前任老闆

第八組題目（電話留言）

給：米勒先生

日期：八月二十一日

時間：下午三點零八分（當你外出時）

來電者：

太平洋通訊公司的湯姆肯先生 / 女士

電話：(253) 555-6736 分機 432

（√）請回電（　）將會再來電

留言：今日的會議已經取消了

Chapter 5 閱讀理解題型題目介紹

傑西先生改期，延至下週一舉行

接線生

李小姐

1. 來電者是誰？

(A) 李小姐　　(B) 湯姆肯

(C) 米勒先生　　(D) 傑西先生

2. 為何來電？

(A) 取消會議　　(B) 確認會議

(C) 通知新活動訊息　　(D) 安排派對

第九組題目（長條圖）

不同雜誌的閱讀率

（調查期間：2009.04～2010.03）

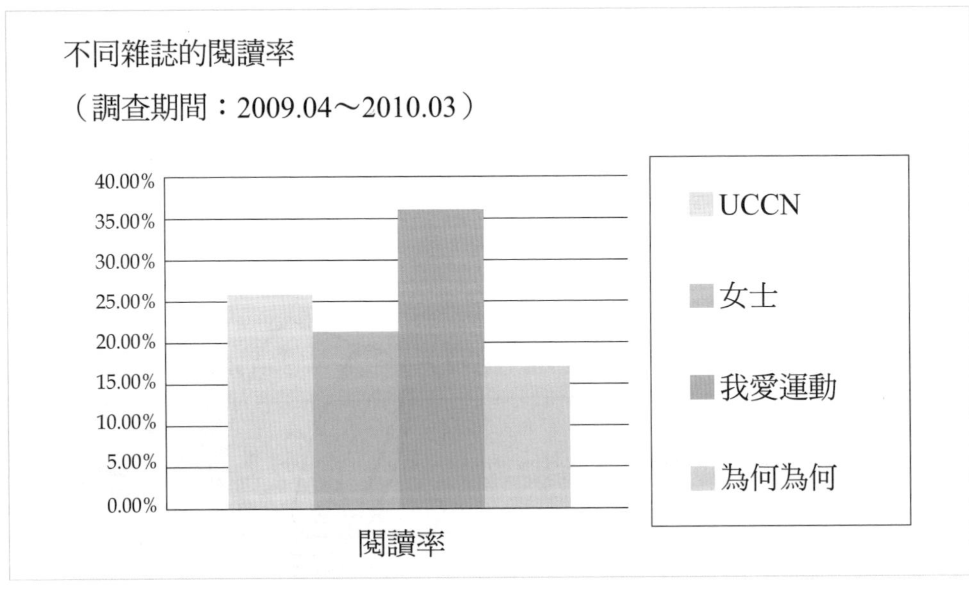

1. 哪一本雜誌有最高的閱讀率？

(A) UCCN　　(B) 女士

(C) 我愛運動　　(D) 為何為何

2. 此圖表涵蓋多久時間？

(A) 半年　(B) 四個月

(C) 一個月　(D) 一年

第十組題目（問卷）

青少年休閒嗜好調查

主題：你空閒時都做什麼？

1. 上網 10%
2. 電腦遊戲 15%
3. 購物 6%
4. 看電視 25%
5. 讀書 30%
6. 做戶外活動 10%
7. 上夜店 4%

1. 青少年最不常的嗜好是？

(A) 購物　(B) 上夜店

(C) 做戶外活動　(D) 睡覺

2. 青少年最常的兩項嗜好是？

(A) 讀書與看電視　(B) 購物與上網

(C) 做戶外活動與上夜店　(D) 以上皆非

第十一組題目（雙篇閱讀：議程與電子郵件）

世界全球公司

部門主管會議

十二月七日週三下午三點半

地點：公司五號會議室

議程

1. 辦公室用品主題
2. 冬季會議計畫
3. 公司尾牙
4. 新的人事規定
5. 檢視去年績效
6. 預算報告

給：安妮塔布列爾
來自：潔思米羅斯瑪莉
有關於：昨日的會議

親愛的安妮塔，
我擔心你的突然病倒。現在好一些了嗎？
昨日的會議進行得很順利，也有準時開始。我們重新安排了議程的順序。我們先討論了第五個項目因為我們都認為去年的績效需要一個很快的檢視，這樣我們就可以在來年發展。這個會議持續兩個小時，而我們沒有時間完成第六項主題。我們設定好了下個月的會議時間，這個會議會包含這一次我們沒有討論到的部分。它將在十七號舉行。同時，因為一些外來的顧問也會參加下一次的會議，我們需要一個大一點的空間讓大家舒適一些。我想五號會議室太小。一號或是三號會是一個較佳的選擇。

快樂喔，
潔思米

1. 哪一個項目最後討論？

(A) 檢視去年績效
(B) 新的人事規定
(C) 辦公室用品主題
(D) 預算報告

2. 會議何時結束？

(A) 3:30P.M.
(B) 5:30P.M.
(C) 4:30P.M.
(D) 2:30P.M.

3. 下一次的會議將在哪裡舉辦？

(A) 五號會議室
(B) 一號或是五號會議室
(C) 一號或三號會議室
(D) 公司自助餐廳

4. 下一次的會議在何時舉辦？

(A) 十二月十七號
(B) 一月十七號
(C) 十二月七號
(D) 一月七號

5. 為何他們沒有討論最後一個項目？

(A) 有一些顧問來了
(B) 沒有足夠的時間
(C) 布列爾女士突然生病
(D) 五號會議室太小

Chapter 6

閱讀理解題型模擬試題二十五組

這一個章節我們將演練閱讀理解測驗題型。由於閱讀測驗的題材多樣性，以下的文章將以各種題材穿插的方式來做演練。其中包括有表格類、書信類與文章類以及雙篇閱讀等的題材。藉由大量的英文文章閱讀，閱讀能力必定將在短期內快速增加。面對實際的考試時便可以因為平常的熟練，而能輕鬆應對。

第一組題目（公告）

SCHOOL'S OUTING

COME AND CELEBRATE WITH US!!

Pizza Palace

No. 48. Park Road. Taipei City

Wednesday, July 27th, 2009.

At 8:00 P.M.

Please reply to let us know how many pizzas we should order.

Thank you!

---

1. Where will you probably see this note?

(A) A company's cafeteria (B) A school's bulletin board.

(C) A bank's website (D) A Pizza house's menu

2. Why does this note ask for a reply?

(A) To make a reservation

(B) To know how many people will attend

(C) To tell where they are going to celebrate

(D) To inform when people can show up at the party

第二組題目（文章－敘述文）

My sister's cat was bit by my dog today and she was very upset about it because it was a gift from her boyfriend. She called me in tears and asked if I could stay with her tonight, and she needed some time to recover from the shock of her cat's frightening experience. I just can't understand why cats and dogs cannot stay together in peace. Maybe it has something to do with their nature. Dogs are active and energetic, while cats are gentle and quiet. When they live together, they certainly have some trouble because of their different life styles. According to some scientific researches in 1900s, scientists even found dogs and cats would release some special odors that make each other sick and uncomfortable. That is to say, they dislike each other's smell and the smell really annoys them. Therefore, next time if you want to raise the two kinds of animals at home, remember to separate them in different places.

---

1. What is this paragraph mainly about?
   (A) Cats are better pets than dogs.
   (B) People can't raise two different animals at home at the same time.
   (C) Scientists did some researches about the smell of human bodies.
   (D) Dogs and cats have trouble living together because of some reasons.
2. According to this paragraph, which statement is correct?
   (A) The author's sister got a dog from her boyfriend.
   (B) Dogs and cats can live together in peace because of their life styles.
   (C) Dogs are full of energy, but cats aren't.
   (D) The author's cat was bit by her sister's dog.

第三組題目（廣告）

Enjoy your Vacation

Feel tired because of your daily hard work? Want to have a vacation and relax yourself? We offer the weekend and weeklong packages just as you want! Stay at an excellent hotel, and enjoy our huge swimming pool, two tennis courts and a private golf court. You will love our nice views and cheap prices. Call 999-276-5673 and make a reservation today!

---

1. What is this advertisement about?

(A) A vacation (B) A mail package

(C) A walking tour (D) An economic situation

2. What can NOT be found in the hotel?

(A) a golf court (B) an exercise room

(C) a swimming pool (D) a tennis court

3. Who might be interested in this AD?

(A) A retired worker who needs a health insurance.

(B) A construction worker who needs to train his body.

(C) An office worker who needs some relaxation.

(D) A student who needs to buy some balls.

第四組題目（電視指南）

TV Tonight

Channel	8:00 P.M.	9:00 P.M.	10:00 P.M.	11:00 P.M.
A	The Game Show	Hollywood Time	Business Time	You and your health
B	Soccer Game	Talk about Money	Love Life	Sports Time
C	News Time	Cooking Time	Arts & Painting	History Talking

1. What is the schedule for?

(A) Tonight's TV programs (B) Transportation timetable

(C) Fashion Show schedules (D) Radio Show schedules

2. What time can you watch a show about Hollywood?

(A) 8:00 P.M. (B) 9:00 P.M.

(C) 10:00 P.M. (D) 11:00 P.M.

第五組題目（私人書信）

To: KK

From: Charlene

Re: Happy weekend is coming!

Dear KK,

Well, finally, it's almost weekend!

What are you going to do this weekend? Do you have any plans? Let me tell you mine first. Tonight, my parents and I are going to the movie. I don't remember the name of the movie, but I know it's a romantic comedy. Then tomorrow, I will have a lot to do, so I won't sleep late. On Saturday morning, I will take a long walk in the park before I enjoy a big breakfast at my favorite sandwich shop. In the afternoon, I will go shopping at Sogo department stores for some new party dresses. At night, I will go dancing with my boyfriend at a disco pub. That's cool, isn't it?

On Sunday morning, I will go to church with my parents. After that, I will go to the beach to meet my friends from college. On Sunday evening, we will all together have dinner in a special Thai food place. Then I will rent some DVDs on my way home and watch them on TV at night. Sounds like I have a busy weekend, right? How about you? Tell me your coming weekend, OK? Write me soon.

Yours,

Charlene

---

1. Why did Charlene write this letter?
   (A) To thank KK for her visiting.
   (B) To give KK some information about churches.
   (C) To tell KK her coming weekend plans.
   (D) To ask KK for her company on the weekend.
2. When did Charlene write this letter?
   (A) Friday (B) Saturday (C) Sunday (D) Monday

第六組題目（傳單）

YOUR SUPER STORE

Weekend's Special Offer

Apples / $35 For A Pound

Watermelons / $28 For A Pound

Cherries / $16 For A Pound

Grapes / $18 For A Pound

Bananas / $10 For A Pound

Wax apples / $50 For A Pound

---

1. What kind of the store is "YOUR SUPER STORE"?

   (A) A stationery store (B) A fruit store

   (C) A vegetable store (D) An appliance store

2. Which one is the most expensive in "YOUR SUPER STORE"?

   (A) Watermelons (B) Bananas

   (C) Apples (D) Wax apples

3. If you buy a half pond of cherries and two ponds of grapes, how much do you need to pay?

   (A) $ 76 (B) $ 34

   (C) $ 66 (D) $ 44

第七組題目（索引）

Books Index

TITLE	PAGE	COPYRIGHT
Successful in Business	57	1983
Be a good manager	88	1987
Get more money at your workplace	90	1998

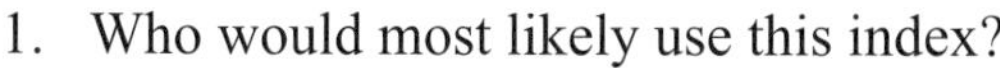
Marketing Management 67 1979

1. Who would most likely use this index?
   (A) Farmers (B) Doctors
   (C) Business people (D) Cooks
2. Which book has the most recent copyright?
   (A) Marketing Management
   (B) Get more money at your workplace
   (C) Be a good manager
   (D) Successful in Business

第八組題目（文章－說明文）

Taking pictures has become part of our everyday lives. For example, people take pictures at wedding, birthday parties and some special events. The technology on taking pictures is also one of the powerful tools. As far as I know, it is used by scientists and doctors for studies.

In 1900, a man named George Eastman invented a new camera, called the "Kodak Brownies". And with the invention of these easy, less expensive cameras, anyone can take pictures. When people want to keep a special moment, the only thing they need to do is just a click. Nowadays, cameras have also created big changes. They allow people to make pictures without films. Moreover, people can show their pictures on their computer screen. In short, modern technology does change our everyday lives a lot.

1. What is the main idea in this article?
   (A) Taking pictures with camera has changed a lot in our everyday lives.
   (B) Computer Science helps people make their pictures changed.
   (C) George Eastman is the greatest inventor in the modern world.

(D) Doctors and Scientists are two largest groups of using camera.

2. On line 9, what does "they" refer to?

(A) Doctors (B) Cameras

(C) Changes (D) Pictures

3. Which one of the following statements is NOT true?

(A) Taking pictures has become part of our everyday lives.

(B) People now can show their pictures on their computer screen.

(C) The first camera is called the "Kodak Brownies".

(D) Cameras are used by scientists and doctors for studies.

第九組題目（徵才廣告）

WANTED

AD

We need you!

If you :

@ Have a master's degree

@ At least 6 years' experience in English teaching field

@ Patient and Love kids

@ Be able to work overtime if there is a need.

Interested please send your information to this email address:

35635@hotmail.com

---

1. What is the purpose of this advertisement?

(A) Courage investment (B) Job opening

(C) Inform a special activity (D) Holiday sale

2. Who would most likely feel interested in this advertisement?

(A) Computer programmers (B) Caregivers

(C) Teachers (D) English translators

第十組題目（索引）

CATALOGUE INDEX

TITLE	PAGE	COPYRIGHT
Corporation and Law	57	1983
Entrepreneur & power	88	1987
Get raises at your workplace	90	1998
Marketing VS. Public Relations	67	1979
Online shopping: Take off!	88	1999
International Trade Forums.	77	1867

1. Who would most likely use this index?

(A) Hotel keepers (B) Online engineer

(C) Business people (D) Airline pilots

2. Which book has the most recent copyright?

(A) Marketing VS. Public Relations

(B) Online shopping :Take off!

(C) Entrepreneur & power

(D) Corporation and Law

第十一組題目（傳單）

TRADE PROTECTION LAWS

Opinions of participates at the 1997 World Trade Convention

In favor of trade without tariffs:

On all products-53%

On automobiles-66%

On raw materials-38%

On paper products-87%

On produce-44%

On manufactured goods-32%

1. What kind of a poll is this?
   (A) Utility (B) Light
   (C) Opinion (D) Census
2. What is the percentage of the participants believe in trading raw materials and produce without tariffs?
   (A) 38% and 53% (B) 44% and 32%
   (C) 66% and 44% (D) 38% and 44%

第十二組題目（文章－說明文）

In North America, the cousin of the typhoon, sometimes called an extra-tropical cyclone or blizzard, is what causes trouble. From January to March, as winter tightens its hold on the central and eastern parts of the North American continent, the risk for blizzards is at the highest level. People living in these areas do what they can to prepare for these paralyzing storms. A blizzard is characterized by winds of 55 kilometers per hour or more, snowfall of at least five centimeters an hour, temperatures near–20 degrees Celsius and visibility of less than a half a kilometer. People caught in a blizzard can be stranded during the storm, as well as after, as they struggle to clear the towering snowdrifts. To prepare for the possibility of blizzards, many people living in central and eastern North America put emergency kits in their cars. During a blizzard, drivers are forced by the poor visibility to pull over and wait out the storm. Some of the things that people stock in the trunks of their cars are blankets, flashlights, batteries and non-perishable food. It's also considered a good idea to include a can and waterproof matches to melt snow for drinking in addition to a shovel, sand, a tow-rope and jumper cables to help you get going again when the storm is over. These kinds of things don't take up much room and they become important for survival in case of an emergency. Thinking ahead when blizzards are a reality saves lives.

1. Where are blizzards a problem?
   (A) On the Pacific Ocean
   (B) On the west coast of North America
   (C) In the central and eastern parts of North America
   (D) Southeast Asia
2. What makes blizzards so dangerous?
   (A) The rain freezes into ice as temperatures drop and the roads become slippery.
   (B) People can be stranded because the limited visibility makes it impossible to travel.
   (C) People can run out of supplies.
   (D) People can freeze to death in the low temperatures.
3. What separates a blizzard from other storms?
   (A) the size of the snowdrifts
   (B) the geographic location
   (C) the speed of the wind, the amount of snowfall and the limited visibility
   (D) the wind comes from the east instead of the west
4. What can people do to ensure that they survive a blizzard if they are trapped in their cars?

(A) keep a cell phone to call for help

(B) avoid traveling during blizzard warnings

(C) keep moving until they outrun the blizzard

(D) keep supplies in the trunks of their cars

5. What does 'non-perishable' mean in this passage?

(A) does not spoil easily (B) light-weight

(C) not difficult to prepare (D) packed in a can or plastic bag

第十三組題目（推薦函）

Wonderland Marketing Company
456 Maple Ave.
San Jose, MA 08965

Sep. 23, 20__

To whom it may concern,

Debbie Abram has worked for Wonderland Marketing Company for the past three years. She started from the bottom as an assistant in the mail room and worked her way up to marketing assistant, in which position she has been working for one and half years.

Ms. Abram is a hardworking, diligent and motivated employee. She is always willing to put in long hours if necessary to have the work done.

She is also an easygoing and energetic person who gets along with her coworkers and supervisors well. During the period of her work, she did some exceptional projects, including the evaluation for the new market in Poston Area and Media Research Program.

Ms. Abram has devoted a lot for our company. We are sorry to lose her because of her moving to a new area and her new career plan. I hereby highly recommend her for any position requiring efficiency, creativity and independence.

Sincerely yours,

Vivian Wang

HR Department, Director

---

1. What kind of correspondence is it?

   (A) a cover letter (B) a resume

   (C) a reference (D) an autobiography

2. What poison does Ms. Abram have now?

   (A) a HR director (B) an assistant in the mail room

   (C) a marketing supervisor (D) a marketing assistant

3. Why will Ms. Abram leave her current job?

   (A) a new plan on her career

   (B) find a better salary

   (C) The location now is inconvenient for her

   (D) discontent with the demotion

4. What does the word in line 2 "Ave." mean?

   (A) Alley (B) Road

   (C) Highway (D) Intersection

5. When was the correspondence written?

   (A) April 5 (B) September 3

   (C) May 2 (D) September 23

第十四組題目（電子郵件）

To : Tony Young

From : May Lin

Subject: New York Trip

Date: January 14, 20___

Tony,

I have to have an emergency trip to our New York office next Tuesday. Please arrange flights and hotels for me. I know this is last minute, but I need to do everything you can help me get it done. I would prefer a morning flight around 7:00AM departing from Boston if you can get one for me. In New York, I like the hotel near the airport better than in downtown since it is more convenient for me. I want a suite in a 5-star hotel with a swimming pool and a fitness room as well. I need to return here on next Friday. Please make these arrangements before the end of tomorrow. Also, e-mail a copy of the itinerary to the manager, Mr. Choi in New York office. I need him to give me a ride when I get to the airport.

May

---

1. Why did May give Tony this email?

   (A) Because she wants him to pick up him at the airport.

   (B) Because she wants him to arrange flights and hotels.

   (C) Because she wants him to go to New York office.

   (D) Because she wants him to stay in downtown.

2. How long is the New York trip?

   (A) 2 days　　(B) 3 days

   (C) 4 days　　(D) a week

3. Who is Mr. Choi?

   (A) Tony's assistant　　(B) May's assistant

   (C) a manager in New York office　　(D) a manager in Boston office

第十五組題目（文章－說明文）

Economists have pointed to the reduction in international flights as a sign that airline industry is in a big financial trouble. This is the most severe situation in this century. The first point cited to support the idea that airline industry is dropping sharply is the recent reduction in the number of passengers. According to the report released last week, the number of passengers this quarter has fallen by 45% over the past three years. This drop represents that over 40,000 workers in airline industry will be retrenched soon. Economists emphasize the situation won't be better until the year of 2017 if the economic situation doesn't bounce back soon.

1. Why do economists think the airline industry may be in trouble?

   (A) The number of passengers is down.

   (B) All workers in the airport will be laid off soon.

   (C) Many pilots decide to resign.

   (D) The rate of air crash is higher.

2. What does it say about the airline industry?

   (A) The economic situation and airline industry will bounce back in the

2017.

(B) Over 40,000 pilots will be retrenched shortly.

(C) Airline industry won't be in trouble until 2017.

(D) The number of passengers this quarter has fallen by 45% over the past three years.

3. When did the report release?

(A) 45 days ago (B) 7 days ago

(C) 2017 (D) three years ago

第十六組題目（新聞報導）

During the past years small supermarkets and grocery stores in the US in the outskirts of big cities have been suffering from a prolonged slump in sales. The reason for that is that superstores and hypermarkets are increasing in number and spreading rapidly. One advantage of superstores is the variety of commodities they are able to carry as they are so large. Additionally, they develop their own house brands. With their own brands, they can offer quality products at 20 percent off name-brand prices, and patrons are always pleased with a bargain.

In order to survive, consequently, local supermarkets and family-owned retail stores are changing tactics by marketing new products with low prices and making their displays more interesting and attractive. Not only are they trying to make a comeback, but they also open new stores located within walking distance of public transportation, once customers walk inside from a station, they can easily find the merchandise they are looking for. What's more, these small retailers also offer customers computer access to a web site that provides the full product line and any related information.

1. What has caused small retailers to alter marketing strategies?

(A) The high rent in outskirts of big cities

(B) The inconvenience location

(C) The superstores are increasing quickly

(D) The severer economic situation

2. According to the essay, what is NOT the small retailers' strategies?

(A) Develop their own house brands

(B) Market new products with low prices

(C) Make their displays more interesting

(D) Offer customers computer access to a web site

3. What does the author indicate about superstores?

(A) They open new stores located within walking distance of public transportation.

(B) They offer customers computer access to a web site that provides the full product line and any related information.

(C) They can offer quality products with cheaper prices.

(D) They can give customers free delivery.

4. What does the word "patron" in this essay mean?

(A) Owners of the grocery stores (B) Clerks in the superstores

(C) Consumers (D) Marketing planners

第十七組題目（電視指南）

TV Guide

TV TONIGHT

CHANNEL 1

6:00~8:00 Politics Today

8:00~9:00 Finance and You

9:00~11:00 Business World

11:00~12:00 Stock Market Today

CHANNEL2

6:00~8:30 Soccer Game: Italy versus France

8:30~12:00 Baseball Game: U.S.A. versus France

CHANNEL3

6:00~7:00 Winning your money

7:00~8:00 Friends

8:00~10:00 Crazy Cops

10:00~12:00 Celebrity

CHANNEL4

6:00~6:30 S*G*T

6:30~7:30 Weather Forecast

7:30~9:30 My recipe

9:30~12:00 Gardening

CHANNEL5

6:00~9:30 Movie: My wedding Day

9:30~12:00 Movie: Who is the murder?

---

1. Who might be interested in Channel TWO?
   (A) People who like sports
   (B) People who like movies
   (C) People who care about money management
   (D) People who like cooking
2. Which channel should you select if you want some gossips about your favorite singer?
   (A) Channel ONE　　(B) Channel TWO
   (C) Channel THREE　　(D) Channel FOUR

第十八組題目（公告－失物招領）

Notice: Lost & Found

1. Lost: A textbook: Introduction to Economics. In the classroom 32. Call 5632-7780. Reward if found.
2. Found: A black wallet. In the library. For details call Chad at 0936-099-677.
3. Lost: English dictionary with name "Peter" written on the cover page. Somewhere on campus. Please call Kiki at 2666-7865.
4. Lost: Gray book bag. Books and a pencil box inside. Possibly left in the laboratory. Please call Holly at 5678-6785 if you find it.
5. Found: A chain of keys. In the parking lot. Call Yoyo for details. 0936-236-786

---

1. Where may you see the notice?

   (A) At school　　(B) At the office

   (C) At the parking garage　　(D) At the clinic

2. Where was the dictionary found?

   (A) In the lab　　(B) In the parking lot

   (C) On the campus　　(D) In the library

3. What are being looked for here?

   (A) A textbook, an English dictionary and a book bag

   (B) A textbook, a black wallet and a chain of keys

   (C) A black wallet, a book bag and a chain of keys

   (D) A textbook, an dictionary and a book bag

第十九組題目（文章－議論文）

The labor movement in the U.S.A. is a topic worth discussing. Many

years ago, working conditions in mines and what we call "sweat factories" were very awful before the efforts of the labor movement in the United States in the 20th century.

Some young children work long hours in the poorly- appointed workplaces instead of going to school, and what is more, they just earned little hour pay. They weren't allowed to take a rest, even to go to the toilet. Some of them speak little English and had trouble expressing themselves well. Of course, they didn't complain too much as they didn't want to be expelled. They need their jobs.

It took a great tragedy to make people realize that working conditions in the U.S.A. were very bad. In 1911, a fire broke out in the Triangle Clothing Factory in New York. The doors to the exit had all been locked so that these workers kept staying at their machinery; as a consequence, the tragedy happened. It was impossible for these workers to escape from the fire, so most people working in that factory died in the terrible fire.

After that, some movements for improvements working conditions took place. For example, some laws required employers to give their minimum hour pay and benefits, and child labor laws prevented young children from working in poor conditions. In addition, in 1971, the Department of Labor established the Occupational Safety and Health Administration (OSHA) to set standards for workplace safety. However, many people think many things haven't been done to the perfect, so people still need to work hard in order to make more goals met.

---

1. According to the article, which of the following descriptions matches a person who works in the "sweat factory"?

   (A) An inspector works eight hours a day in the factory.

(B) An assembler works from 8:00 AM to 5:00PM with a sixty-minute break during the lunchtime.

(C) A construction worker works hard and perspires a lot in the construction site.

(D) A cleaner has no time to have lunch or take a rest.

2. Which of the following words can replace the word "expel" in the article?

(A) terminate (B) explore

(C) retire (D) warn

3. Why was the organization "OSHA" built?

(A) To make laws to stop crimes.

(B) To be a bridge between the labor unions and enterprisers.

(C) To insure the safety in different workplaces.

(D) To record the success and failure about antisocial activities.

4. Why is the author say "people still need to work hard in order to make more goals met"?

(A) Because the labor movement is a constant process.

(B) Because they are lack of volunteers.

(C) Because employees don't get a raise annually.

(D) Because the government still has no laws to protect labors under 12.

第二十組題目（商業書信－備忘錄）

Memorandum

Date, August 7th, 2010

To: Debbie Kou, assistant

From: Harry Wang, director of Information System

Re : Your great ideas and my next week itinerary

Debbie,

Thank you for your suggestion about recycling our unused computer equipment. After I read your proposal, I think we have plenty of equipment that may be useful to students in our school district. Just like you said, many of our computers are still in good working order even though they no more fulfill our needs. In exchange for our computers, some schools want to offer us some awards and that should be good for our reputation.

Another thing, I will go for an important conference on Internet Marketing next week in Japan. Can you please arrange the air ticket and hotel reservation for me? I think I will stay in Tokyo Comfort Inn for three nights. (I don't like the suite you arranged for me last time. I want a double occupancy this time.) Also, I need someone to pick me up at the airport when I am back in Taipei. Thanks in advance.

Harry Wang

Director of Information System

GMP

---

1. Why did Harry Wang send this memo?

   (A) To confirm his itinerary.

   (B) To offer his suggestions.

   (C) To ask for hotel arrangement.

   (D) To thank Debbie for her computer donation.

2. What does the word "reputation" mean?

   (A) Investment

   (B) Fame

   (C) Business

   (D) Reservation

3. Which of the following statements is NOT true?

(A) Harry wants a double room instead of a single room.

(B) Harry needs to go to Japan for a conference.

(C) Many computers in GMP are still in good conditions.

(D) Harry will go to Japan by aircraft.

4. Who is Debbie Kou?

(A) Harry Wang's assistant.

(B) Harry Wang's travel agent.

(C) A member of the faculty at school.

(D) Director of information system in GMP.

第二十一組題目（文章－說明文）

Dance can be regarded as old as human civilization. People dance for many different reasons. For instance, people danced for rain to grow their crops. They dance for certain weather conditions. People danced for good hunting and good health, too. Before they went hunting, they usually danced as a pray for God. Even warriors and soldiers danced, too. They often danced to feel brave and have more energy.

Dancing plays an important role in many festivals in the world. Like the people of Central and South America celebrate a holiday called Carnaval. They dance "Samba" to celebrate the holiday. People in China and Japan also dance on important holidays. They dance a traditional dance called "the Dragon Dance". Many new dances have appeared over the last 200 years. In the 1800s, "Waltz" became very popular among western people. "Tap dancing", another type of dance, is a combination of American, Irish and English dances was also a mainstream. In the 1950s, rock 'n' roll created "Disco", and now "Street Dance" is popular because we have rap music.

1. Which of the following reasons for dancing is NOT mentioned by the author?
   (A) For rain to grow crops.　　(B) For good hunting.
   (C) For more courage.　　(D) For good wealth.
2. Which type of dancing is popular with people before "Tap dancing"?
   (A) Waltz　　(B) Disco
   (C) Free Style　　(D) Street Dance
3. Which country celebrates "Carnaval"?
   (A) China　　(B) Japan
   (C) Brazil　　(D) America

第二十二組題目（網頁廣告）

Web Page

DONATE

Thank you for your interest in the Disabled Foundation of Taipei. We are a nonprofit organization registered with the Official Charities of Taiwan.

ONLINE DONATION

If you want to contribute your money, you only need a click. Please fill out the attached form and remember to note your credit card number and the amount you want to donate. If you don't want to use your credit card, we suggest that everyone donate funds in person or by mail. No amount is too small. Strong city starts from a dollar you donate. After you donate your money, you will receive your receipt within two weeks, and you can keep the receipt and place it in your tax file.

GET INVOLVED

VOLUNTEER

DONATE

1. Where may you see this?

(A) A notice on the school board.　(B) A web page on your computer.

(C) A text message.　(D) On your receipt.

2. Which of following statement is correct?

(A) Disabled Foundation is a profit organization.

(B) You need to mail your money order if you want to make a donation.

(C) You need to donate at least a certain amount of money.

(D) You can have a receipt in order to file your annual tax file.

第二十三組題目（雙篇閱讀－徵才廣告+信函）

We Want You!

Top public relations company is seeking a senior publicity person to join our team of PR. If you a creative and energetic team worker as well as a senior in this field over five years, then you are the person we are looking for. Must have a Master's in Business Administration or Psychology, and have knowledge of Statistics a plus. Have a good command of English, including four parts of skills, listening, speaking, reading, and writing. Please send your cover letter, resume, autobiography and three letters of reference to Peter Kovacs, Director of Human Resources, Howard Public Relations, 4521 State Street, Suite 256, Springfield, YT 5826. Closing date is May 15th.

Mary Wade

56 Trend Street, Apt.98

Hilton, RT 45640

Dear Mary Wade,

Many thanks for your letter dated May 14th regarding your interest in our company. Unfortunately, the position we offered had been filled when we got your letter. However, because of your excellent education background and work experience, we might be interested in considering you for a position in the near future. Your resume shows that you have the education level we ask, and you also have more years of experience in the field than what we require. I am really interested to know you more because we studied in the same university. I would keep your resume on file and contact you when we have another position available.

Sincerely,

Peter Kovacs

Director of Human Resources

Howard Public Relations

---

1. Who wants a job?

   (A) Mr. Kovacs (B) Ms. Wade

   (C) Hilton (D) Howard

2. Where does Peter work?

   (A) A public relations company (B) A university

   (C) An English institute (D) It doesn't say

3. What degree does Mary have?

   (A) A doctorate degree (B) A master's degree

   (C) A bachelor's degree (D) A high school degree

4. What requirement is "NOT" needed for this job?

   (A) Good English ability

   (B) Be active and full of imagination

   (C) Have learned about business or Psychology

   (D) Over five-year experience in the field of law affairs

5. Which is "NOT" needed when apply for the job?

(A) Cover letter (B) Letters of recommendations

(C) Autograph (D) Resume

第二十四組題目（雙篇閱讀－課程表+電子郵件）

English-LANGUAGE INSTITUTE
CLASS SCHEDULE

English Conversation

LEVEL	DAY	TIME	TEACHER
Basic	Mon. & Fri.	7:00-9:00P.M.	Charles
Elementary	Tue. & Thur.	7:30-9:30P.M.	Viola
Intermediate	Wed. & Fri.	7:00-9:00P.M.	Max
Advanced	Mon. & Thur.	8:00-10:00P.M.	Ryan

English Grammar

LEVEL	DAY	TIME	TEACHER
Level 1	Mon. & Fri.	9:00-10:00P.M.	Helen
Level 2	Tue. & Thur.	7:30-9:30P.M.	Grace
Level 3	Wed. & Fri.	9:00-10:00P.M.	Sue
Level 4	Mon. & Thur.	6:00-8:00P.M.	Alex

English Writing

LEVEL	DAY	TIME	TEACHER
Argumentation	Tue.	7:00-9:00P.M.	Charles
Description	Mon.	7:30-9:30P.M.	Vivian
Narration	Fri.	7:00-9:00P.M.	Tony
Business Letter	Sat.	8:00-10:00P.M.	Ian

Classes begin on the first Monday of every two months. Each class lasts two months. Tuition is $245 per class. To register for classes, please come to our school.

Our address is : 895 Milton Boulevard. Midtown ,YU20154

To: K.M. Jackson

From: Mimi Ting, Director, HR Department.

Re: Language Training

Mr. Jackson,

I've reviewed your application and attached the class schedule, and I think it would indeed give you some useful language skills for your work. English classes in that institute are reputable. I recommend that you start from Intermediate level. It starts at 7:00P.M., which would give you half an hour to get there after you leave work. It's not far from the office, just on the corner of Main and Maple, so that's plenty of time. English grammar is also very important. You know we still make some mistakes while speaking at times, so I suggest the level 3 class for you. Also, please be acknowledged that the company will cover all the tuition for you, so you don't need to worry about it.

Best regards,

Mimi Ting

HR Department

---

1. What time does Mr. Jackson leave his work?

   (A) 5:30P.M. (B) 6:30P.M.

   (C) 7:00P.M. (D) 7:30P.M.

2. How many days a week does the language school provide?

   (A) 4 (B) 5

   (C) 6 (D) 7

3. How can students register the class?

(A) Make a phone call (B) Mail a letter

(C) Mail an application form (D) Come there in person

4. How much should Mr. Jackson pay for the tuition for these two classes?

(A) 245 (B) 490

(C) 0 (D) It doesn't say

5. Who teaches three days in this institute?

(A) Mimi (B) Charles (C) Viola (D) Mr. Jackson

第二十五組題目（雙篇閱讀－帳單+信件）

Contacting Phone Company

Date: June 28th, 20___

User's Name: J.R. Bold

Address: 78 Ice Avenue, Baltimore, TY 67532

Client Number: 555-673-907

Last month's Account Summary

Amount of last bill: $77.78

Due Day: May 16th

Your payment: $80.00

This month's charges

Residential Line(201-555-9933)	**$44.21**
Unlimited answering service	**$8.34**
Long Distance	**$0.00**
State and local tax	**$7.77**
Subtotal	**$60.32**
Credit	**-$2.22**
TOTAL:	**$58.10**

To access your phone messages, dial your home number and enter your password. Any billing questions, call our toll-free number: 1-777-555-7867. Enter your client number after you call. Please have your phone bill on hand in order to make the inquiry smoothly.

Thank you.

Contacting Phone Company

78.Yellow Ave. Suite 567

Maple town UX.67776

Dear Contacting Client,

From your last phone bill, it appears that you have switched to another new long-distance telephone company. We understand our clients' choices and would appreciate having another chance to get our business back! Following please be acknowledged that this month we offer our current clients some incredible low prices when you have a long-distance call. Unlimited calling anywhere in the world, only $59.00 per month for weekdays and $65.34 per month for weekend.

Meanwhile, you will be automatically in our monthly lucky draw. You will have a chance to get a luxury sedan and an SUV. Further questions? Call our Customer Service Hot Line:1-777-888-3647.

Contacting Phone Company always cares and contacts you!!

---

1. Why did the phone company send J.R. Bold this letter?
   (A) To remind him to pay his overdue charges.
   (B) To convince him to use their long-distance again.
   (C) To inform him to get a prize because of winning a lucky draw.
   (D) To remind him to pay this month's phone bill.
2. What number should J.R. Bold call if he has some concerns about billings?

(A) 555-673-907 (B) 201-555-9933

(C) 1-777-555-7867 (D) 1-777-888-3647

3. Which of the following is true about J.R. Bold's May bill payment?

   (A) He didn't pay it.

   (B) He was charged some overdue fees.

   (C) He paid $77.78.

   (D) He paid more than necessary.

4. What should J.R. Bold do after he calls the toll-free number?

   (A) Pay enough tolls

   (B) Enter 555-673-907

   (C) Call Customer Service Hot Line

   (D) Enjoy the monthly lucky draw

5. What does "residential line" mean?

   (A) Home phone (B) Bad connection

   (C) Text message (D) Cellular phone

閱讀理解題型模擬試題二十五組解答

第一組				
1	2			
(B)	(B)			
第二組				
1	2			
(D)	(C)			
第三組				
1	2	3		
(A)	(B)	(C)		
第四組				
1	2			
(A)	(B)			
第五組				
1	2			
(C)	(A)			
第六組				
1	2	3		
(B)	(D)	(D)		
第七組				
1	2			
(C)	(B)			
第八組				
1	2	3		
(A)	(B)	(C)		
第九組				
1	2			
(B)	(C)			

第十組				
1	2			
(C)	(B)			
第十一組				
1	2			
(C)	(D)			
第十二組				
1	2	3	4	5
(C)	(B)	(C)	(D)	(A)
第十三組				
1	2	3	4	5
(C)	(D)	(A)	(B)	(D)
第十四組				
1	2	3		
(B)	(C)	(C)		
第十五組				
1	2	3		
(A)	(D)	(B)		
第十六組				
1	2	3	4	
(C)	(A)	(C)	(C)	
第十七組				
1	2			
(A)	(C)			
第十八組				
1	2	3		
(A)	(C)	(D)		

第十九組				
1	2	3	4	
(D)	(A)	(C)	(A)	
第二十組				
1	2	3	4	
(C)	(B)	(A)	(A)	
第二十一組				
1	2	3		
(D)	(C)	(C)		
第二十二組				
1	2			
(B)	(D)			
第二十三組				
1	2	3	4	5
(B)	(A)	(B)	(D)	(C)
第二十四組				
1	2	3	4	5
(B)	(C)	(D)	(B)	(B)
第二十五組				
1	2	3	4	5
(D)	(C)	(D)	(B)	(A)

筆記頁

筆記頁

筆記頁

筆記頁

筆記頁

國家圖書館出版品預行編目資料

瞬間理解英文閱讀／陳頎著. --初版. --臺北市：書泉, 2013.10

面； 公分.

ISBN 978-986-121-857-1（平裝）

1.英語 2.讀本 3.學習方法

805.18 102016888

3AC3

瞬間理解英文閱讀

作　　者— 陳　頎

發 行 人— 楊榮川

總 編 輯— 王翠華

主　　編— 溫小瑩　朱曉蘋

執行編輯— 吳雨潔

封面設計— 吳佳臻

出 版 者— 書泉出版社

地　　址：106台北市大安區和平東路二段339號4樓

電　　話：(02)2705-5066　　傳　　真：(02)2706-6100

網　　址：http://www.wunan.com.tw

電子郵件：shuchuan@shuchuan.com.tw

劃撥帳號：01303853

戶　　名：書泉出版社

總 經 銷：朝日文化

進退貨地址：新北市中和區橋安街15巷1號7樓

TEL：(02)2249-7714　　FAX：(02)2249-8715

法律顧問　林勝安律師事務所　林勝安律師

出版日期　2013年10月初版一刷

定　　價　新臺幣280元